Highest Praise for Leo J. Maloney and his thrillers

For Duty and Honor

"Leo Maloney has a real winner with *For Duty and Honor*—Gritty and intense, it draws you immediately into the action and doesn't let go."

—Marc Cameron

Arch Enemy

"Utterly compelling! This novel will grab you from the beginning and simply not let go. And Dan Morgan is one of the best heroes to come along in ages."

—Jeffery Deaver

Twelve Hours

"Fine writing and real insider knowledge make this a must."

—Lee Child

Black Skies

"Smart, savvy, and told with the pace and nuance that only a former spook could bring to the page, *Black Skies* is a tour de force novel of twenty-first-century espionage and a great geopolitical thriller. Maloney is the new master of the modern spy game, and this is first-rate storytelling."

—Mark Sullivan

"*Black Skies* is rough, tough, and entertaining. Leo J. Maloney has written a ripping story."

—Meg Gardiner

Silent Assassin

"Leo Maloney has done it again. Real life often overshadows fiction and *Silent Assassin* is both: a terrifyingly thrilling story of a man on a clandestine mission to save us all from a madman hell bent on murder, written by a man who knows that world all too well."

—Michele McPhee

"From the bloody, ripped-from-the-headlines opening sequence, *Silent Assassin* grabs you and doesn't let go. *Silent Assassin* has everything a thriller reader wants—nasty villains, twists and turns, and a hero—Cobra—who just plain kicks ass."

—Ben Coes

"Dan Morgan, a former black-ops agent, is called out of retirement and back into a secretive world of politics and deceit to stop a madman."

—The Stoneham Independent

Termination Orders

"Leo J. Maloney is the new voice to be reckoned with. *Termination Orders* rings with the authenticity that can only come from an insider. This is one outstanding thriller!"

—John Gilstrap

"Taut, tense, and terrifying! You'll cross your fingers it's fiction—in this high-powered, action-packed thriller, Leo Maloney proves he clearly knows his stuff."

—Hank Phillippi Ryan

"A new must-read action thriller that features a double-crossing CIA and Congress, vengeful foreign agents, a corporate drug ring, the Taliban, and narco-terrorists… a you-are-there account of torture, assassination, and double-agents, where 'nothing is as it seems.'"

—Jon Renaud

"Leo J. Maloney is a real-life Jason Bourne."

—Josh Zwylen, *Wicked Local Stoneham*

"A masterly blend of Black Ops intrigue, cleverly interwoven with imaginative sequences of fiction. The reader must guess which accounts are real and which are merely storytelling."

—**Chris Treece,** *The Chris Treece Show*

"A deep-ops story presented in an epic style that takes fact mixed with a bit of fiction to create a spy thriller that takes the reader deep into secret spy missions."

—**Cy Hilterman,** *Best Sellers World*

"For fans of spy thrillers seeking a bit of realism mixed into their novels, *Termination Orders* will prove to be an excellent and recommended pick."

—Midwest Book Reviews

Also by Leo J. Maloney

Termination Orders
Silent Assassin
Black Skies
Twelve Hours
Arch Enemy
For Duty and Honor
Rogue Commander
Dark Territory
Threat Level Alpha
War of Shadows
Deep Cover
The Morgan Files
Angle of Attack
Hard Target
Storm Front
Blast Wave
Enemy Action

The Morgan Dossier

Leo J. Maloney

LYRICAL UNDERGROUND
Kensington Publishing Corp.
www.kensingtonbooks.com

To the extent that the image or images on the cover of this book depict a person or persons, such person or persons are merely models, and are not intended to portray any character or characters featured in the book.

LYRICAL UNDERGROUND BOOKS are published by
Kensington Publishing Corp.
900 Third Avenue, 26th Floor
New York, NY 10022

First Electronic Edition: October 2024
eISBN-13: 978-1-5161-1-2036 (ebook)
ISBN - 13: 978-1-5161-1211-1 (Print)

149853405

DARK TERRITORY

CHAPTER ONE

Alex Morgan was lying face down on a hillock of freezing Russian snow.

She had been there for more than two hours, barely moving, and now her body was starting to rebel. It didn't matter that she was stuffed in a cocoon of polypropylene thermals, Icelandic socks, Sorel mountain boots, a bone-white Gore-Tex suit and a polar bear Inuit hat. The temperature had dropped to minus eight degrees Celsius. She felt like one of those wooden sticks wrapped in an ice cream bar.

Suck it up, Morgan, she told herself as she tried to stop her teeth from chattering. *Just make the shot.*

To her left and right were lines of enormous pines, the edge of the forest from which she'd crawled. Their branches speared upwards into an inky sky, needles barely fluttering in the windless night. Below her, out front, the hillock dropped off into waves of avalanche snow before smoothing out at the bottom across a vast plain of unmarred white—maybe three kilometers across and surrounded by more pine-crested hills. A couple of trees in the snow bowl were bent under coats of gleaming ice.

It looked like a scene from *Dr. Zhivago*, an old movie her father, Dan Morgan, liked—except she wasn't watching it next to Dad on a couch. She was in it, up to her neck.

The first sound that reached her frozen ears was a thin, distant squeal, like someone turning a rusty pump handle. Then came the rumble of a piston engine. She squinted as a track-equipped Sno-Cat vehicle emerged from between two faraway hills on the right and started inching to the center of the snow bowl. Then, from the left, a Russian ZiL military truck appeared, crawling cautiously forward as well.

Game on, Alex thought as she reached to her left with one Gore-Tex glove and carefully slipped the white tarp from her rifle. She glanced up at the sky, where a frothy filigree of clouds was splitting at the center—revealing a huge, glowing, perfect orb. Her teeth stopped chattering, and she smiled.

Alex loved a sniper's moon.

A day earlier, she'd arrived in Vladivostok aboard a ZIM Lines tramp steamer—a 650-foot container vessel that had six berths for adventurous passengers. Zeta Division analysts knew that Russian border controls at the ports were tight, so she'd come off the boat with nothing but her US passport, visa, winter clothes, and a backpack containing her photographic gear. No weapons but a ceramic, undetectable Benchmade boot knife.

From there she'd found her way to a prearranged safe house, where she picked up her sniper-hide clothing, rifle, ammunition, and rangefinder. Then she'd moved to a second garage location, scooped up her motorcycle, and headed north for Razdolnoye—a nothing little town on the road to Ussuriysk.

She'd had Lincoln Shepard talking in her ear comm—using GPS back in Boston and satellite overheads—to get her off the main road at Razdolnoye, twenty klicks west, and then here to this snow-cone hill. She'd hauled all her gear, plus a pair of short skis, up through the forest as the night fell, hard and cold. Then she'd said good-bye to Linc, pulled the comm out, and stripped the battery. Her dad had taught her that. If Linc sneezed at the wrong time, he could screw up her shot, and she wasn't going to get a second chance.

The Sno-Cat and the ZiL were approaching each other toward the middle of the snow bowl. Alex rolled to her right, popped the top of her snow suit open and pulled a Sig Sauer Kilo rangefinder monocular from the relative warmth of her chest. She rolled back onto her stomach, pushed her snow goggles up on her white fur hat, and peered through the scope.

The Russian ZiL's windows were all frosted up. She couldn't tell how many men were in the cab, but that didn't matter. It was an old Soviet vehicle, which she knew was manned by rebel Ukrainians. In the back, under the canvas cover, was Satan's pitchfork, a high-yield tactical nuke lifted from Ukrainian military inventory.

The Sno-Cat's windows were heated and clear, and she could plainly see four figures inside. One of them was Colonel Shin Kwan Hyo of the Democratic People's Republic of Korea. Pyongyang had just tested its latest long-range ballistic missile, the Unha-3. It couldn't carry a heavy payload, such as the bulky North Korean atomic warheads, but it had a range of ten thousand kilometers. Pop a compact tactical nuke in the nose cone, and the DPRK could take out Los Angeles. Alex thought the Hollywood whackos could use some pruning, but not this way.

In a couple of minutes those two vehicles were going to meet, and the world's power balance would irrevocably change for the worse.

She figured Colonel Hyo would be easy to spot. He'd be the one carrying a briefcase, or satchel, of cold, hard cash. Plus, she had a very clear image of his face in her mind. Lily Randall had described exactly what he looked like—thick arching eyebrows, black eyes, a flat nose, and a white scar to the left of his thin lips. It was the face that had sneered down at Lily for hours while Hyo tortured the hell out of her in China. Lily was Alex's friend—a very close friend. Alex only wished she could send Hyo a good-bye note along with her bullet.

The vehicles slowed to a stop, facing each other at twenty meters—engines idling, exhausts blowing steam in the air. Their occupants started to get out, forming a small cluster in the glow of the headlights. Alex pressed the rangefinder trigger—730 meters, or 2,395 feet, with a downward angle of five degrees. It would be a long shot, just at the end of her rifle's effective range. Could she do it? Damn straight she could, but now she had to move fast.

She slithered to her left through the snow and got behind her Accuracy International Arctic Warfare. It was a beautiful weapon in lime green furniture, with a free-floating stainless steel barrel, and a Schmidt & Bender 6x24 PMII variable magnification scope. And hers was the special-ops version, with a folding stock and suppressor. She pulled the glove covers off her fingers, adjusted the bipod, popped up the scope covers, and nestled the beast to her cheek. It felt like being kissed by an ice cube.

Alex didn't need a range card. She'd memorized every possible variable, which was sort of amusing since she'd been so lousy at math in college. Maybe it was a matter of motivation. She started running calculations in her head as she peered through the scope, worked the bolt quietly, and seated a round in the breech. Linc had told her the rifle would already be zeroed; he'd better have been right. And she'd warned him to tell the armorers not to clean the barrel afterward; a pristine barrel could give you an off-the-mark, cold bore shot.

Okay, M118 Special Ball ammo, 7.62×51mm, range at 730 meters . . . That'll mean a bullet drop of minus seventy-nine inches. Zero wind, so no lateral adjustment. Got to compensate for the suppressor, which slightly increases muzzle velocity, so kick the bullet drop back up to minus seventy-eight inches.

She reached for the scope's elevation knob and turned it, counting off minute-of-angle clicks, which tilted the front of the scope downward. This meant that when she set the crosshairs on Hyo's face, her barrel would actually be tilted up, shooting at a spot six-and-a-half feet above his head. Gravity would pull the bullet down precisely that much and, hopefully, ruin his life.

She pulled the scarf up over her nose so her lung steam wouldn't fog up the scope and pressed her eye socket to the rubber ring. Her heart rate picked up, thumping through her suit against the hard pack snow. The shapes of five men filled her reticle, huddled close and talking. The two on the left were Ukrainians, easy to spot by their leopard camouflage, fur hats, and AK-47s. On the right were two North Koreans in full-body black ski suits—also slinging weapons—but she couldn't tell what kind. In the middle, facing her, was a broad-shouldered man wearing a long winter coat—collar turned up—and a fur hat with the ear flaps snapped skyward. Next to his right boot a dark briefcase sat in the snow. But was that Hyo?

Then he lifted a gloved hand to his lips, one of the Ukrainians extended a fist, and a cigarette lighter flamed up. His face glowed yellow as he dragged on the cigarette, blew out the smoke, and smiled. Nice white scar, right next to his snarling lips.

Wait! She remembered she'd have to compensate for the five-degree downward angle. *Okay, Colonel John Plaster's drop table . . . I'll have to hold low . . . Five degrees means multiply seventy-eight drop inches by point zero zero four . . . uhh . . . hold low on the target by a third of an inch. Aim for the throat.*

Her hands were trembling. By pure force of will, she sent what was left of her body heat into her fingers, balled them into tight fists, and slowly released. Better. She turned the scope's magnification ring and filled the reticle with Hyo's ugly face, sitting it right above the vertical crosshair post. She slipped her right thumb into the rifle's thumb hole, curled her fingers around the icy grip, and barely touched the trigger, easing it past the first stage until she felt the secondary pressure.

Hyo was laughing at something, his black eyes open to the sky as his lung steam poured from his mouth. *Laugh it up, mofo*, Alex thought as she inhaled a breath, released it halfway, and held it. Her entire body stilled except for one thing: her trigger finger.

She heard her dad's voice in her head: *"Don't squeeze the trigger with your finger. Squeeze it with your mind. And always let the shot surprise you."*

Squeeeeze...

The crosshairs jumped as the bullet left the barrel and the butt pad bucked her shoulder. Because of the suppressor, the only sound the rifle made was like a closed-mouth sneeze, and there was barely a flash. Alex stared through the scope. A second went by, then another. Hyo pulled the cigarette from his mouth. Then his head exploded.

Alex didn't wait. She knew the rest of those men were in shock, slimed with Hyo's blood and brain matter, and scrambling to bury themselves in the snow or to haul ass back into their vehicles. She shifted her shoulders to the right, cranking the barrel left, and took a bead on the ZiL's cargo bed as she worked the bolt. She fired again. While that round was still in the air, she put one more down range. If she was lucky, a round might hit the nuke warhead. It wouldn't set it off, but it would make it useless.

She quickly shifted left, swinging the barrel to the right toward the Sno-Cat. Now she could hear thin, panicky shouts echoing from the surrounding hills, and the Sno-Cat was roaring backward. She laid her crosshairs two feet behind the moving cab, squeezed off another shot, and then raised her head up, both eyes open. The Sno-Cat's side window shattered, and it skittered across the snow like a drunken ice skater.

Enough.Time to get the hell out of Dodge.

She snapped her scope covers down, her bipod up, jammed her rangefinder into her Gore-Tex suit, and slithered backward into the tree line—leaving a gouge in the snow like a sea turtle's tail. She rolled over, sat up, swung the rifle behind her, shoved her arms in the double slings, and staggered upright. She was breathing hard now, almost panting with the adrenaline surge, and then she heard the first gunshots. They sounded wild, un-aimed, which made sense since her suppressor had masked her location. Then a short AK-47 burst sliced off some branches just above her head.

Okay ... wrong!

She took off, tramping downhill through the maze of black pine trunks. The forest was about a hundred feet deep, but then it ended at the head of a five-hundred-foot slope—the snow gleaming in the moonlight, marred only by her own footprints from her climb uphill. Her short skis were right where she'd left them, sticking up like a pair of rabbit ears. She yanked them out, slipped her boots into the old-fashioned cable bindings, pushed off hard, and squatted low as she heard more gunshots whip-cracking through the trees above and behind her.

She made a dead-straight run down the hill, no turns, picking up so much speed she wasn't sure she'd be able to stop. Then she spotted the low mound of hand-shoveled snow with her signal twig jutting up. She sat hard on her left buttock and skidded in, showering a plume of snow.

She kicked off her skis, got up, and hurled them away as far as she could. Then she shoved her gloves in the snow mound up to her elbows and grunted hard as she hauled herself backward. Up popped a Ural 750cc Russian motorcycle—the Sahara model, sand tan with a black engine. She'd already named it.

"Come on, Natasha," Alex whispered as she jumped on, cranked the ignition, and stamped on the starter. "Growl for me, baby!"

The engine did as she asked, and Alex hunkered low, twisted the throttle, fishtailed onto the icy road, and sped off like a demon back toward Razdolnoye.

* * * *

By the time she got close to the bridge over the western vein of the Razdolnaya River, she had her ear comm fired back up, and Linc was talking to her.

"You should see it coming up in about one klick," he said. "Looks like an old British Bailey bridge."

"I see it," said Alex as she took a swipe at her snow goggles. "You picking up any radio chatter, Linc?"

"Negative. I don't think the Ukes and the NKs will be complaining to the Russians. Did you pass any traffic?"

"One truck," Alex said as she slowed the bike on the bridge. The heavy steel structure was perched about fifty feet above the river, its roaring black water peppered with swirling ice floes. "If the driver saw my rifle, he probably thought I was out for some biathlon practice."

Linc laughed. "Diana's very pleased, by the way."

"Good."

Linc hesitated, but he just had to ask. "What'd you feel when you hit him?"

"Recoil," Alex said. She got off the bike, looked around, and stamped the kickstand down. "I hate this part, Linc," she complained.

"Just do it," he said. "It's only a tool. We'll buy you a new one."

"Yeah, but not *this* one."

She unslung her rifle, kissed it, and leaned through the girders. Then she let it go and watched it slowly spinning down through the darkness. She waited until it made a tiny splash and disappeared. Then she pulled out her rangefinder and got rid of that too.

"Done," she said.

"Outstanding," Linc said. "Get crankin'."

An hour later, she pulled into the outskirts of Ussuriysk. She was exhausted, shivering, and hungry. Her last two Power Bars hadn't done much, and she'd finished all the water in her pocket flask. Thankfully, Linc was with her, so she didn't have to navigate or think much. He guided her along the snow-shouldered streets of the small Russian town, past one pretty church with gleaming red onion-spire caps, and then into the mouth of a dark, slimy alleyway that had frozen bedsheets crackling from clotheslines strung across the apartments above. Two blocks down at the end of the alley, she could see the back of a tavern that must have been a hundred years old.

Alex stopped the bike and dismounted. "Guess it's time to dump Natasha too."

"Don't worry about her," Linc said. "She'll get recycled."

"Is that a pun?"

"Sort of."

She stripped out of her sniper cocoon, fur cap, and goggles, leaving her dressed in a blue-black Mountain Hardwear jacket, jeans, and boots. She found a garbage can that reeked of rotten fish and stuffed everything deep inside, including her sniper gloves—they'd be covered with gunfire residue. Then she pulled a back pack from the Ural's saddlebag, rummaged past her photography gear, slipped into a pair of girlie-pink woolen gloves and matching ski cap, whispered "Thanks" to Natasha, and walked.

"How's my train timing?" she asked Linc as she clipped along the alleyway.

"Perfect. It's just pulling in from Vladivostok. But those things can sit in the station for two hours or be gone in five minutes. Better hustle."

Alex walked faster as the rear service door of the tavern loomed. She yanked it open and strode right through the steam-fogged kitchen, where a couple of Mongolian cooks stared at her. Then she pushed through the doors and into the tavern. It was long and dark, filled with rough-hewn tables and benches, with a heavy wooden bar on the right. The place was packed with nothing but men, and in one corner, a balalaika musician strummed Russian folk songs. His half-in-the-bag audience sang along while their beers slopped over their tankards.

Alex walked up to the bar, where a huge man with a Santa Claus beard was just bringing a large shot of vodka to his lips. She snatched it out of his hand, threw her head back, and swigged the entire thing down. Then she grabbed his beard, kissed him wetly on his merry red cheek, and said, "*Spaseebah*!"

"*Pajalstah*!" The big man laughed. His belly jiggled as Alex marched right past his approving comrades and out the front door.

The train station was nothing—just one small stop on the Trans-Siberian's 9,289-kilometer trip from Vladivostok to Moscow. There was only one small ticket building, closed for the night, but she already had her ticket. Her dad had told her long ago that you never went near an airport after a hit. Trains were much easier, and the conductors could be bought if you had to.

The Trans-Siberian was just pulling in to the platform. The locomotive was a hulking steel box with a blazing light up top, two glass windshields for eyes, three red stripes across its face, and a big red Soviet star for a nose. The follow-on cars were long and silver and lined with curtained windows. The first passenger car stopped in front of her, and its door slid open. Nobody got off, and there were no other passengers on the platform. A conductor leaned out, wearing a long green woolen coat and a fur hat. He looked like a Stalin relic.

"Passport," he said in heavily accented English.

Alex smiled her college girl smile and handed it up, along with her ticket. He looked at them both, glanced at her backpack, and handed them back.

"Where you come from, young woman?" he asked.

"Vladivostok."

"Um-hmm. And your profession?"

"I'm a funeral photographer."

His thick eyebrows furrowed. "What is that?"

"It's like a wedding photographer, except the groom doesn't move."

He cocked his head and smiled. "Welcome to Russia."

She got on.

CHAPTER TWO

The long, low, whistle of the train's locomotive woke Alex from a slumber of the dead.

She blinked at the compartment's ceiling, unsure of exactly where she was. Then she felt the vibrations, and heard the comforting clacks of iron wheels turning, so she released the breath she'd been holding—along with the strands of a nightmare about whistling bombs falling from the sky. It was weird how real-life sounds could slither into your brain and darkly feather the edges of a dream.

She raised her head and looked around. She was lying on a brocade divan that doubled for a bed, and was covered by a thick, maroon, down quilt. First things first; she slipped a hand under her pillow, found her Benchmade blade, then pulled the coverlet off and sat up. She was still wearing all her clothes, except for her boots, and barely remembered making her way to this compartment's bed. It was almost like having a hangover, except she'd only been drunk on action and adrenaline—both of which were exhausting after the fact.

Pretty nice digs, she thought.

The sleeping compartment was small—Second Class, not First—but had all the accouterments that a bachelorette sniper needed. Her bed faced another across the way, which was piled with ornate pillows. Below the large, rectangular window was a ceramic-topped table—neatly piled with soft drinks, water bottles, and snacks, all labeled in Cyrillic. The thick, closed drapes kept the compartment bathed in a soothing golden hue, but when she reached over and flicked one aside the morning sun stabbed her eyes. She squinted hard and turned away. Apparently she'd slept all night, which was a rare treat for a person in her business.

Alex reached for a water bottle, twisted the cap off, and took a long, cool swig. Only then did she pull the ear comm from her backpack, switched it on, and pushed it deep in her auditory canal.

"Morning, Petunia," said Lincoln Shepard's cheery voice.

"Jesus," said Alex. "You stalking me? I haven't even had coffee yet."

"Caffeine's bad for shooters. Gives you the shakes."

"I'm off duty. Where am I anyway?"

"You're on a train." Linc almost snickered.

"Wise guy."

"Actually, you're approaching Khabarovsk, arriving at 09:10 local time for a twenty-five minute stop."

"Can I go shopping?"

"No. Wanna know how long this whole schlep takes?"

"If you must."

"It's about 2,500 miles from Vladivostok to Irkutsk, total travel time seventy-one hours. You've only knocked off about ten so far."

"Oh God," Alex moaned. "I'll go out of my mind."

"Read a book. You've got a full day today, then another tomorrow, and an arrival time of 16:47 on the third day. After that you've got another 1,500 miles to Omsk, and that's your exfil into Kazakhstan, but we'll have no comms for most of that."

"What do you mean? Why not?"

"There's a patch of about a thousand miles where that train's in dark territory—no cell towers anywhere, or uplinks from the engineer's cab. So you better not need me for anything."

"Did I ever?"

Linc didn't laugh at that, which was the sign he was about to get serious.

"And one more thing, Alex."

"Shoot."

"Ugh," he grunted. "Interesting choice of words for you. Anyway, we swept that train for chatter, and there's nothing coming up about your most recent activities. However, Russia House says there's somebody aboard using a satellite phone."

Zeta Division didn't have a full complement of translators, but instead used contractors formerly employed by the NSA. Hence, the "Russia House" moniker.

"A satphone, huh?" Alex mused. "Maybe the user's a ham radio hobbyist."

"Yeah, or FSB. So watch your six."

"Roger. Can I go get breakfast now?"

"Bon appétit. And enjoy your R&R, Alex. Have to admit, I'm just a bit jealous. I heard tell that the Trans-Siberian has some breath-taking views."

"If I see any, I'll let you know. After emerging from the D.T., of course." She could practically hear him smile as she pulled the comm out, wiped it with a tissue, and returned it to her backpack. Then she pulled on her boots, slipped her ceramic blade inside the right one, and was just about to go grub-hunting when she caught a glimpse of herself in the compartment's oval mirror.

That's nasty, she thought as she examined her unwashed hair. She hadn't showered in days. Her stomach growled. *Shut up,* she admonished. *You can wait.* She pulled a thick towel from the suitcase shelf above the bed, scanned the compartment once to make sure she wasn't leaving anything revealing behind, shouldered her backpack, and went out.

The ladies' was at the end of her train car, along a slim corridor lined with tall windows. A rush of bucolic Russian farmscape flashed by in waves of yellow wheat, and the car rocked side-to-side like a tugboat floating on easy swells. As she made her way, a man smiled and flattened himself against the windows to let her pass. He was a rather handsome Russian in a black turtleneck and brown woolen blazer, with swept-back blond hair and fashionable glasses. She smiled in return, a little embarrassed at her unwashed state.

The ladies' had a tiny shower stall. She locked the door, stripped, squeezed in, pulled the curtain, and nearly screamed when the freezing water hit her like an arctic waterfall. She broke her shampoo and rinse record—finishing in under a minute—then toweled off roughly and fast. She switched to a fresh bra, boy shorts, and socks, then jumped back into a cream cable sweater and her jeans. Finally, she put her boots back on. She wiped off the foggy mirror, peered at her face, and decided that the blush of youth required no makeup. With a quick finger-combing of her hair, she went out to follow the scents of breakfast.

The Trans-Siberian railway was a throwback to the steamships of old, with various classes and appropriate décor—depending upon one's culture and status. The trains were long, usually comprised of ten cars or more, some of them ancient enough to still have slat wooden floors. At the back, of course, were the Third Class cars—packed with Chinese and Siberian peasants sitting on slat benches reminiscent of church pews. These were hardy folk who could endure hours of having their rumps bruised.

Center to the trains were the Second Class cars, commonly populated by foreign tourists or middle-class Russians, most of whom paid for sleeping berths. When they dined, they sat facing each other on padded seats across polished tables, in meal cars that resembled upscale urban diners. Finally, up front were the First Class accommodations, where the wealthy reposed in suites of bed chambers and sitting rooms, and dined in plush rolling restaurants whose chefs and wait-staff could compete with New York's Russian Tea Room at its prime.

All of this was mildly interesting to a twenty year-old who'd dropped out of college to become a special operations agent for Zeta Division. Dan Morgan—her father, mentor, and, at times, tormentor—had instilled in her a curiosity for classical lifestyles, all the while preparing her to mirror his experience as a former CIA agent. But as far as classics were concerned, Dad's fascination ran more to finely tuned automobiles than cellos, so Alex had an appreciation for the curves and sheens of well-made transportation vehicles. And this train was *damn* pretty.

But Alex would not be distracted by her current plush environment, as she'd learned to regard every enclosed structure, mobile or not, as a potential trap from which to escape. She didn't care much for the fact that she'd be stuck on the Trans-Siberian for days, especially given the hit she'd just pulled off. She'd have to remain super vigilant, and, as she made her way forward in search of the Second Class dining car, she had her ear comm on again, her cell phone in her hand, and her boot knife ready to be drawn.

As the train rolled into a screeching stop at Khabarovsk, she passed through the connector and into another berthing car, where she stopped to gaze out the windows. The station was nothing more than a long concrete slab butting up against a small station house and a row of newsstands and tourist trinket shops. The conductors had hopped down to help oncoming passengers with valises, while a throng from the train spilled out to snatch up whatever they could buy—probably the morning newspapers, snacks, and those Russian nesting dolls that now featured Vladimir Putin as top dog.

Alex pushed on through the next "submarine" chamber and into the Second Class dining car, where a waft of sausage and eggs nearly made her swoon. The car looked like an Italian bistro plucked from Milan, with gleaming wooden tables lining both flanks, leather-backed bench seats, green brocade window curtains with tasseled sashes, and a curved ceiling of timber beams and tiffany lamps.

At the far end was a half-circle serving bar, behind which a pretty blonde attendant in a Caribbean blue suit worked the juice and coffee machines. The car was half-full of diners stabbing at steaming eggs and fresh fruit. Alex plunked herself down at the first empty table on the right, facing the distant bar, and shortly thereafter, the train began rolling again.

"Good morning, Miss Alex."

She looked up to find her "Stalin" era conductor from the night before gazing down at her. Without his long woolen coat and fur hat he looked even more like the old dictator, with a drooping moustache and thick grey hair combed back from his forehead. Now he was wearing an olive tunic with a leather cross-strap and money pouch. She smiled up at him.

"Good morning to you, Sasha," she said.

He raised a bushy eyebrow.

"How do you know this is my name?"

"You said it was Alexander, last night, when you took me to my berth. Isn't Sasha the nick-name for Alexander?"

He wagged a thick finger at her. "You are very smart, for an American."

"*Spaseebah*." She dipped her head.

Sasha grunted and moved on to check the tickets of the newly-boarded. But the encounter chilled her a bit. He'd remembered her first name, so he probably remembered the family name on her passport as well: Morgan. She was using her bona-fide, government-issue document, a practice which, in the old days of espionage, would have been totally verboten. But ever since the advent of social media, the traditions of "cover" for intelligence agents had become more complex.

A girl her age would have to have a Facebook page, replete with pics of herself and her "friends." If she was using a phony name and got pinched, any cyber warrior worth his salt would do a deep reverse-image search and she'd be up the creek, no paddle. So sometimes, especially with a quick hit, you had to play it straight and hope for the best. Her father, being an old school spy, hated these new trends of the Great Game.

The waitress in blue took her breakfast order, then Alex toyed with her cell as she watched two men enter the car through the door past the bar. The first was huge, with a muscle builder's physique under a waist-length black leather jacket, sunglasses, and tight blond curls— maybe forty years old. The man behind him was ancient and bent, wearing a long woolen coat and walking with an old-style wooden cane. They took a booth near the bar on the left, with the big man's back to her and the old man's face in full view.

He reminded her of someone; then she smiled inside as she remembered. Peter Conley, her father's best friend and currently an agent with Zeta, had a poster in his office cubicle of Albert Einstein, the famous physicist. It was a totally out-of-character shot, with Einstein sticking his tongue out. This man had exactly that look—wild white mane, merry blue eyes—but without the pink appendage. For some reason, she subtly snapped a picture of him with her cell. Maybe she'd show it to Conley later for a laugh.

As the waitress delivered her mango juice, coffee and scrambled eggs, Alex was taken aback as a man slipped into her booth. It was the same guy who'd flattened himself against the windows earlier to let her pass.

"*Dobroyoutra,*" he greeted her with a charming smile.

"*Dobroyoutra,*" Alex returned. "*No yaneegovoryupo-russki.*"

He cocked his head to the side. "You seem to speak it very well."

"Only enough to get myself in trouble."

The man chuckled, then extended his hand.

"I am Uri Yankovski."

Alex took it. His grip was firm and warm, and it was clear he was going to hold hers until she gave up her name.

"Alex."

The waitress rescued her by arriving with her food. Uri smiled up at her and said, "The same," in English, then added, "but tea for me if you please."

He folded his fingers on the table and offered a nod at Alex's plate. She dug into her eggs and watched his face.

"Are you a tourist, Alex?" he asked.

"I'm a photographer, actually."

"How interesting."

Alex raised her coffee cup to her lips, but kept her eyes on his.

"Are you a spy, Uri?"

He jerked his head back and laughed, but she caught the twitch at the corner of his eyes. Her father had taught her that: use an apparently innocent verbal ambush, then ignore the protests and watch for the telltale signs. He was a spy all right, probably FSB, the modern version of the KGB. Or maybe GRU, military intelligence.

"What makes you ask that?" he said.

She raised one shoulder. "Oh, I don't know. You look like one of those dudes from the Jason Bourne flicks."

He waved a dismissive hand. "No, I am simply a boring accountant."

"Of course." She jabbed a sausage with her fork and bit off the end.

The waitress returned with Uri's breakfast. He carefully unfolded a white cloth napkin onto his lap and joined Alex in devouring eggs.

"So, Alex," he said between bites. "When do you plan to get off?"

"That's a rather personal question." Another trick of the trade from her dad. Hit him with an idiom and you'll find out quickly how deep his language skills are. If he gets it, he's probably spent lots of time in the States. But Uri didn't, and his handsome forehead creased.

"It is? I apologize ..."

"Irkutsk." Alex smiled again as she lied. "I might shoot something from the windows, but mostly I plan to relax."

"Very good. I am also going to Irkutsk."

I'll bet you are, she thought. *Or anywhere else I say that I'm going.* She wondered if he'd been set on her tail due to the Hyo affair, but somehow she didn't think so. If he were really after her, he wouldn't have gone anywhere near her, or even smiled at her back at her car.

Just then Sasha came back through the dining car, and when he saw that she was sitting with a man, he gave her an admonishing grandfatherly look. She returned it with an expression that said, *It's not my fault I'm cute*, and he passed by with his nose turned up.

"Well, it's a long ride," said Alex as she finished her breakfast and dabbed at her lips with her napkin. "Maybe we'll cross paths again." As she shouldered her backpack and slipped out of the booth, Uri raised himself up an inch in politeness.

"That would be pleasant," he said. "I have heard they play cards here at night."

"Be careful with me," she said. "You might lose your shirt." With that, she turned and headed back to her berth, hoping for a very boring, very restful, three days of nothing.

* * * *

The meal took its toll, as well as the previous long mission nights with keyed-up nerves and no sleep. She slept for another two hours—on her back with her head on a brocade pillow, stocking feet facing the door—covered up with the quilt, but loosely gripping her knife underneath. It was a delicious nap, like being rocked in a cradle, with the sounds of the clicking train wheels and warm winter light seeping through the closed curtains.

But around 1:00 pm, she snapped her head up, fully awake. Her sliding door was locked, but someone outside was turning a large iron key in the hole. The door hissed open and Sasha the conductor stepped inside. He closed the door and stood there staring down at her, with a very strange expression on his slabby face.

"What is it, Sasha?" Alex sat up on her elbows.

"That man that you ate your meal with," he said in a heavy whisper.

"Yes?"

"He is dead."

CHAPTER THREE

Spartan kicked Dan Morgan in the groin.

The blow, delivered with the top of her foot where the laces criss-crossed her boxing shoe, lifted him off his feet about an inch and gushed a grunt from his lungs. Thankfully, he was wearing a cup under his suit, but the blow surprised him. It surprised her too.

"Why'd you let me do that?" Spartan demanded in an accusatory tone. She stood back and jammed her fists to her hips, with a hard rubber training blade clutched in her right hand. Her spiky blond hair looked particularly wild today, and she was wearing black spandex leggings and a cut-off black tee, showing her muscled arms coiled with tattoos.

"I didn't *let* you," said Morgan as he winced and re-adjusted his cup. "I screwed up. Thought you were going to use the knife."

"I was, but you've got a blade too." Spartan rolled her eyes. "You're the one who's always telling us if you see a blade, use your feet first." She jutted her square jaw at his duds. "I think it's that suit. You can't fight in a tie."

"Oh really?" Morgan cocked his head and twirled his own training blade in his fingers. "Seems to me I *also* told you to always train in your street clothes. Think you're gonna have time to jump in a phone booth and switch to that Super Girl outfit?"

"What's a phone booth?"

"Never mind." Morgan got himself back into his fighting stance while he snorted, "*Kids*."

Spartan did the same, leading with her left foot, and she instantly brought her right knife hand up in an overhead arc and started to lunge. But Morgan charged her, KravMaga style. He twisted to the right while launching his left shoulder hard into her right collar bone, snapped his left arm up under her knife arm to trap it, and slammed his right knee into her solar plexus. She bent over with a hiss as he speared his right elbow down on the nape of her neck, whipped his knife hand under her head, raked his training blade across her throat, and dropped her on the mat, facedown.

"Damn it!" She cursed as she pounded the mat with a fist.

"See?" Morgan stood over her, grinning. "Never underestimate your elders. We're sneaky."

The gym door opened, and Diesel stuck his head inside. He'd been letting his brush-cut black hair grow longer, gelling it back, which made Morgan think he'd been watching episodes of *Mad Men.* Diesel looked down at Spartan and back up at Morgan.

"Hate to screw up your Twister tournament, but we're wanted in the War Room."

"Now?" Spartan looked up from the mat. "I was just about to get revenge."

Morgan sneered down at her. "You talk a good game for a corpse."

"On the double, Morgan," Diesel said. "There's a fire and your daughter's been playing with matches."

Morgan jerked his chin back. The last he'd heard, Alex had pulled off a nice clean hit and was on the Trans-Siberian, headed for an easy exfil. Something had clearly gone off the rails, but he was careful to never let his teammates at Zeta Division see his fatherly concerns. So he just gripped Spartan under her armpit and hauled her up.

"Okay, let's hustle," he said as he took Spartan's knife as well as his own and dropped them in a large copper urn, where all sorts of fighting implements were jammed inside like deadly umbrellas.

The three operatives quick-marched past the rows of analyst cubicles and into the War Room, where Zeta Division chief Diana Bloch and her director of operations, Paul Kirby, were already ensconced in their head-honcho leather chairs at the right side of the large circular conference table. Across the way, Peter Conley was tipped back in a chair, reading the morning's *Boston Globe* and resisting the urge to cross his flying boots on the tabletop. To the left, Lincoln Shepard was hunched over his Alienware laptop, wearing the ever-present white Bluetooth headset that seemed grafted to his skull. At Shepard's elbow sat Karen O'Neal, Zeta's top analyst and Shepard's not-so-secret paramour.

Morgan grabbed a chair across from Conley, while Spartan and Diesel found other seats. Morgan and Conley had worked as operational partners at CIA for more than two decades before coming over to Zeta. They had a mind-meld thing going and Morgan wanted to be able to see Conley's eyes. He glanced up at the War Room's curved ceiling, where a large skylight displayed a phony blue sky. Above that, a flock of Canadian geese cruised by with light honks and languid flapping. In about twenty minutes, the same geese would fly by again.

"Close the door and hit the countermeasures, Diesel," Diana Bloch murmured as she perused a report.

Diesel jumped up, pulled the door, pressed a button on the near wall and a light hum permeated the space. The War Room was a multi-million dollar SCIF, or Sensitive Compartmented Information Facility, designed to defeat all types of electronic surveillance. This one was also wired for sound so all briefings could be recorded. Diana looked at her watch.

"Non-standard briefing," she said to no one. "Oh nine hundred hours, sixteen April, two thousand eighteen." She looked over at Paul Kirby. "Take it, Mr. Kirby."

Kirby pushed his wire-rimmed glasses back up over the bump in his nose and cleared his throat. "As of last night, Agent Morgan …" He looked over his glasses at Dan Morgan and added, "*Junior* … was clear and mobile aboard exfil transportation, traveling west in the UTC-plus-nine Russian zone. However, an encounter with an unknown factor appears to have exposed her to some scrutiny."

Diesel raised a finger. "What's UTC?"

Kirby frowned at the interruption. "Universal Time Coordinated."

"It's like Zulu time for civilians," Peter Conley said to Diesel.

"Diana," Morgan said, "can we get this brief in plain English?"

Kirby's faced flushed and he leaned forward to defend his turf, but Diana waved him off.

"All right," she huffed as she dropped her file folder. "Alex pulled off her mission very well and boarded the Trans-Siberian last night, her time. This morning, two things occurred. One, while at breakfast in a dining car, she spotted a passenger who gained her interest and she captured his image. Two, she was joined at breakfast by a man we now believe was an FSB agent. However, that encounter appeared to have been of a passing interest nature, initiated by him."

"What do you mean, passing interest?" Spartan asked.

"He liked her," Diana said.

"So he hadn't made her," said Morgan.

"Sounds like he *wanted* to make her," Diesel quipped. Morgan shot him a glare and Diesel raised his hands and said, "Sorry, bro."

"So far," said Peter Conley, "doesn't sound like much of an emergency."

"I'm not finished." Diana skewered Conley with one of her warning glances. "Apparently, this FSB man is now deceased."

"Jesus," Morgan groaned.

"Oh boy," said Conley. "Murder on the Orient Express."

"Did Alex take this guy out?" Morgan asked Diana.

"Negative," said Shepard. He was tapping away on his laptop, but as always he was able to split-brain his tasks—fully engaged in a conversation while working. "She left him in the dining car, went back to her berth and was informed after the fact by the train conductor."

"Any name on the dead dude?" Conley asked.

"Introduced himself to Alex as Uri Yankovski," Shepard said. "Probably a cover."

Diana gestured at Karen O'Neal. "Run that, Karen." O'Neal pecked at her own laptop.

"Why'd the train conductor inform Alex about this guy's demise?" Morgan asked Shepard.

"Because he'd just seen her breaking bread with him in the dining car. There's also one railroad cop on the train—standard procedure—he and the conductor took Alex to a toilet where they'd found the corpse. She did her squeamish college girl act, insisted that she didn't know the guy, and that he'd probably just had a heart attack. But she says his eyeballs had burst vessels and she smelled walnuts. The conductor and the cop put him on ice and sent her back to her bunk."

Peter Conley looked at Morgan and said, "Walnuts."

Morgan nodded. "Somebody made Uri eat cyanide."

"Shepard," Diana said, "let's see that image."

The War Room's semi-circular wall monitor glowed with Alex's iPhone photo of the elderly man in the dining car booth. Of the large man facing him, only a slice of the back of his head and one shoulder could be seen.

"Hey, that's Albert!" Peter Conley laughed.

"Albert who?" Diesel's brow furrowed; he was trying desperately to keep up.

"Looks just like that poster of Einstein in my cubicle," Conley said. "But without the tongue."

"That's why Alex took the shot," Shepard said. "But it turns out the resemblance goes deeper than just face."

"Just brief it and dispense with the theatrics, Shepard," Paul Kirby sneered. He had to say *something* or become utterly superfluous.

Shepard's cheeks reddened, but he complied and carried on. "That man is Dmitry Kozlov, age seventy-six, and until just recently a top-level aerospace scientist with Russian Space Command. Kozlov's crowning achievement was the design and deployment of a communications satellite called Laika II, still in orbit. But the satellite's actually a camouflaged MIRV platform."

"What a merve?" Spartan asked.

"Multiple Independently Targeted Reentry Vehicle," Shepard said. "In other words …"

"A bunch of nukes they can drop on our heads whenever they want," Conley cut in.

"That's right," Shepard said, "but it gets better, or worse, depending on Kozlov's intentions. The old man's daughter was Svetlana Kozlov, an independent journalist, and no fan of the current Kremlin regime. She was doing a bunch of corruption stories for the *Financial Times*. Putin's thugs murdered her a couple of months ago, and right after that, Kozlov was forced to retire."

Conley emitted a long low whistle, like a bomb falling from the sky. "So, we've got ourselves one pissed off, elderly, genius mourner."

"And perhaps a perfect target for defection," Paul Kirby offered.

"All alone on a train, with Alex," Diana added. "Could be an opportunity."

"He's not alone," Dan Morgan muttered. He was staring intently at the monitor, his dark eyes narrowed like lasers.

"I've got a make on Uri Yankovski," said Karen O'Neal. She spun her laptop around to show everyone the image on her screen. It was a surveillance shot of Yankovski sitting at a European café somewhere and looking much like he had on the train with Alex. "It's a cover name; real name Sergei Tolstoyev. But he wasn't FSB; he was GRU."

"Military Intelligence," Diana said. "Makes sense. They're afraid Kozlov's trying to defect or escape, so they put someone on him from inside Defense."

"No," Dan Morgan said flatly. He was still squinting at the image of Kozlov and seemed to be mentally drifting, but he softly snapped a finger at Lincoln Shepard and said, "Can you crop in closer on the guy he's with?"

"There's nothing much there, Cobra," Shepard said. "Just the back of his …"

"Give it to me." Morgan's tone was sharp and unyielding.

Shepard worked his magic and the monitor filled with a blurry image of curly blond hair and one ear. Then he slewed his cursor, clicked and tapped, and the image became crystal clear. No one else in the room spoke as Morgan rose from his chair and leaned across the table, staring.

"What up, bro?" Conley asked with concern as he followed Morgan's gaze. "You look like you've seen a ghost."

"I have," Morgan muttered, then pointed. "See that thick white scar on the back of his upper ear? I gave it to him."

"Explain yourself, Morgan," Diana snapped.

He turned to her and splayed his palms on the table. "That's not just some muscle Kozlov hired to help with his baggage," Morgan said. "That's Maxim Kreesat, a.k.a. the Ghost. He's a former officer with an outlawed Serbian special forces team called the Shadows, now freelance mercs. The two of us once had a heated argument, with knives." He looked back up at the monitor. "And now he's on a train, with Alex."

"That's simply a coincidence, Morgan," Kirby huffed, then huffed again when Conley couldn't manage to restrain a disbelieving laugh.

"Yes," Diana agreed unconvincingly. "Whatever he's doing on that train with Kozlov, it has nothing to do with Zeta Division or …"

"What Alex's extraction plan?" Morgan interrupted as if Bloch had been spouting nonsense syllables.

"She is scheduled to debark at Omsk," Kirby said. "From there, an asset is taking her into Kazakhstan. We've negotiated her exfil with the Chinese; General Kung, to be specific. Nothing could be more secure, Morgan."

"If she makes it that far," Morgan said, but he was ignoring Kirby and focusing only on Bloch. "What do you always say about coincidence, Diana?"

"That there is no such thing."

"That's right. Cancel the Chinese gambit. I'm going to get her myself."

"The hell you are," Kirby snorted.

Morgan turned on Kirby with a look that threatened to set his balding head on fire. "Think of it this way, Paul. Whatever happens to Alex, happens to you next."

Kirby shrunk back in his chair. "Insubordination is highly …" But then he trailed off.

Morgan turned back to Diana. "I'm either going over to Logan right now and catching the next Aeroflot, or you're giving me Conley, the Gulfstream, and Linc to cover my ass. Your call."

Diana sat back and thought, while five pairs of operative and analyst eyes blinked at her like those of begging children. Paul Kirby had warned her numerous times about hiring the daughter of a top agent, but she hadn't listened, and now it had come to this. She could fire Morgan right there and then, but he'd still go off on his own. And who could blame him? At least keeping him partially tethered was always better then letting him completely off-leash.

"All right." She ignored Morgan's expectant glare and turned to his lifelong partner. "Conley, take this fretting parent, and Mr. Shepard as well, and go warm up your jet."

CHAPTER FOUR

Maxim Kreesat's ice blue eyes were like those of a veteran surgeon, appraising each man, first, by the texture of his skin, then his estimated density of bone, and finally his ability to survive the scalpel.

Kreesat relaxed on a red brocade couch inside one of the First Class suites that lined the forward cars of the Trans-Siberian railroad. He held a black Balkan Sobranie cigarette in his karate-calloused fingers, and regarded the old man across from him through spirals of pungent smoke. Dmitry Kozlov, looking small and rumpled in a matching armchair, gazed out the compartment's window at the blur of scenery rushing by, his age-mottled right hand absently turning the shaft of his walking cane.

"It is time to discuss our arrangement, Doctor," Kreesat said in Russian. The Ghost and his Serbian Shadows team had been trained by Russian Spetsnaz officers, so his language skills were sufficient, if a bit crude. Under the Russian commandos' tutelage, he had learned to operate as a cross-continental chameleon; he also spoke English, French, and German quite well.

"As we agreed, Mr. Kreesat," Kozlov murmured without turning his head. "You shall ensure my escape to the West, and, whatever the American reward might be, you will receive half of that." The old scientist's white curls trembled a bit with the rhythmic clacks of the train wheels.

"I am afraid that will not be enough," Kreesat said. "The Americans are not very generous with defectors."

Kozlov turned from the window, his aging green eyes glistening. He'd been thinking of his precious daughter, Svetlana, seeing her as a child once more. The painful reminiscence had filled his eyes. "I am a scientist, Mr. Kreesat, not a man of means. I have nothing more to offer you."

Kreesat smiled, an expression that touched only the curl of his thick lips. His top front teeth were implants, having lost the originals to a Croatian rifle butt. "Ah, but you do, Doctor." He dipped his eyes at the breast pocket of Kozlov's threadbare tweed jacket.

Kozlov's trembling left hand rose to touch that same spot. "Without these disks, I am nothing," he said.

"I only wish to borrow them, and with your expert help, use them for a certain effect. Then you may have them back."

Kreesat glanced through the open doorway that led to the berth's sleeping compartment, where the only female member of his team, Amina, sat on a bed, dressed in neon-blue bobsledder's tights and a matching turtleneck. She had the body of a wrestler, the elliptical eyes and flat nose of a white leopard, and she was preening a Gerber tactical knife on a whetstone, a vision that stirred something in Kreesat's loins. The other five members of his team, all men, were ensconced in an adjoining suite.

"Borrow them?" Kozlov reached for the cup of black tea on the table between them, but it had gone ice cold, and he withdrew his hand. His ancient heart thumped against the small case inside his jacket, where a pair of mini-disks contained all the encrypted operational codes to the nuclear satellite, Laika II.

"Yes, we'll call it a life-saving loan." Kreesat leaned forward and dropped his burning Sobranie into the tea, where it hissed like a cobra. "You understand, Doctor, that defection is a long, arduous process. The Americans will take months analyzing your disks, whereupon they will most likely claim they are useless, in order to deprive you of a just reward. However, my plan is to offer them a small demonstration, after which the value of your disks will increase a thousand fold."

"What sort of demonstration?" Kozlov reached up and fingered the saggy folds beneath his chin.

"We will remove the satellite from its current orbit and re-task it. First, it will cruise above Washington D.C., and then, Moscow."

Kozlov shook his white-maned head. "That is impossible without certain equipment. I do not have the means to do this."

"Ah, but I do," Kreesat said. "Right here, aboard this train."

Kozlov, whose wizened body had begun to squirm, now froze in his chair and stared at the Serbian mercenary. "You have multi-band microwave equipment *here*?" He twisted his head around as if he'd missed such an obvious thing, then looked at the Ghost again. "What are your intentions, Mr. Kreesat?"

"To demand compensation, up front."

"From whom? The Americans?"

"Yes, and perhaps from the Kremlin as well."

"But they will refuse!"

"In that case, you will arm one of the nuclear warheads aboard Laika II, and make its trajectory known."

"No, no." Kozlov raised both small hands and started waving them in front of his face, as if warding off a demon. "I only wish to reward the Americans with what I know, and thereby punish Moscow."

Kreesat cocked his granite head. "For the loss of your daughter."

"Yes, for Svetlana." Kozlov's eyes began to fill up again.

"You valued her above all else."

"She was my greatest blessing… a golden child."

"And Moscow must pay for their crimes."

"Yes, but not like this. I will not…"

Kreesat reached into his leather jacket, removed a smart phone and laid it face up on the table between them. Then he folded his calloused fingers and regarded Kozlov as if he were jungle prey.

"Are you healthy, Doctor?"

"What?" Kozlov had opened the top button of his flannel shirt.

"Your heart. Have you had any previous medical difficulties?"

"No." The old man was completely confused now, his bushy eyebrows cleft into furrows.

"Good. Then look at me, carefully, and calm yourself. I am going to relay some news that may be a shock."

Kozlov slumped in his chair. He placed his mottled hands on his knees and waited.

"Your daughter, Svetlana," Kreesat said. "She is not dead."

Kozlov's sagging cheeks flushed, and his breathing quickened. "What do you mean?"

Kreesat smiled. "She was not murdered by Putin's FSB thugs. She disappeared. Evidence was found of a struggle, including her blood, and an assumption was made by all the media, as well as yourself. Correct?"

Kozlov, speechless, only nodded.

"She was abducted, Doctor. She is being held in captivity so that you will comply with certain demands. And for the time being, she is perfectly healthy."

Kozlov looked like he was going to pass out. His mind filled with the precious images of his beloved daughter, and the horrific emotions of loss and revenge that had turned his respected life and career into a living hell. His eyes overflowed, and his small hands balled into fists.

"But who would do such a thing?" His voice rose to a trembling pitch. "Svetlana was abducted by *whom*?"

Kreesat tapped the screen of his smart phone, then tipped it up from the table, displaying a full screen photo to Kozlov. It was an image of Svetlana, sitting in a chair, her fingers gripping a copy of *Pravda.* The newspaper's date was only three days old.

"By me, Doctor," Kreesat said.

Kozlov bent over and vomited up his cold tea.

* * * *

Alex dropped to one knee and adjusted her shoelace.

She was in the train corridor outside Kreesat's suite, and her posture was merely cover for something she had to do quickly. An hour before, while still back in her Second Class berth, she'd switched her boots for running shoes, slipped her knife inside her jeans at the small of her back, picked up her digital SLR camera and gone on the hunt.

The footwear switch was another technique she'd learned from her dad. An errant lace always served as a good excuse to pause on the move, check your surroundings, upset the flow of a tracking team or, as in this case, plant a bug.

For awhile she'd cruised the length of the train, occasionally stopping to click her shutter at something from a window, or capture an interesting curve of locomotive architecture. But foremost in her mind was the information that had just been relayed from Lincoln Shepard. The man she'd dined with before his cyanide demise had indeed been a Russian intelligence agent. The old Einstein guy was a bereaved Russian aerospace scientist with a bone to pick, and defection on his mind.

And the big blond muscle dude was no Guy Friday to Dmitry Kozlov—he was Maxim Kreesat, a Serbian killer-for-hire and an old nemesis of her dad. And he probably wasn't alone.

All of that was mildly interesting, though unrelated to her hit on Colonel Hyo, and it hadn't fazed her until her father decided to play the "white knight" to her "damsel in distress," which she sure as hell wasn't. But whenever he got his panties in a wad about her safety, there was no stopping him, and now he was jetting her way with Peter at the Lear controls and Linc probably gripping the arms of an aircraft seat and praying. It was all so annoying. The only way she'd ever be allowed to come into her own was if her dad was retired or dead—perish the thought.

But after hearing what she'd heard from Linc, she wasn't going to do as ordered and just sit in her berth and wait for the cavalry. It was still a long, long way to Irkutsk. And since she'd been hired by Zeta as an intelligence operative, that's what she intended to do: operate.

Up front in one of the First Class cars, while she was clicking away at some Russian cows, Kozlov and Kreesat had finally strolled past her and entered one of the suites, along with a girl who reminded her of a throwback Soviet version of Spartan. Then, five more deadly-looking males, including one frigging giant, had appeared and gone into the adjoining suite. This Kreesat guy had a crew.

That's when she'd first used Daddy's shoelace technique—strolling casually down the corridor, taking a knee at the wall of Kreesat's suite, and quickly taping her ear comm to the bottom wall with a Band-Aid. Then she'd risen, walked another ten feet down the corridor, squeezed one of the car windows down into the sill and started photographing more cows again. But in fact, she hadn't seen anything through her viewfinder.

The SLR was embedded with a short range receiver and audio recorder, linked to her ear comm, which could be used as a listening device. So, for half an hour, she'd seen nothing more than a spectrum of audio waves dancing in her viewfinder on a small LED screen, which assured her the comm was picking up gold. At that point, her operative instincts had told her to gather her toys and withdraw.

Now she was down on one knee again, ripping the Band-Aid and comm off the bulkhead wall, stuffing both in her jeans pocket and strolling away for good. Behind her, she heard Kreesat's door slide open, and the hairs on her nape started prickling. But she just kept on walking, feeling cold eyes on her spine.

Four cars down, she reached her own berth, popped inside, locked the door and leaned back on it, releasing a long slow breath of relief. She glanced at the bottle of mineral water on her table.

I should have bought vodka in the bar, she thought. *This kinda stuff could make a girl age fast.*

She sat down on her bunk, pulled her ear comm out of her jeans pocket, stripped it off the Band-Aid, wiped it on her jeans and stuck it deep in her ear.

"You copy me, Linc?"

"Five by five," his tinny voice answered, with a rush of jet engine wash in the background.

"Where you at?" she asked.

"Who knows? I'm just a dog in the passenger seat, but I figure we're closing fast."

"Okay, whatever," she said. "I'm going to shoot you up something from my Canon."

"That sounds vaguely dirty," Linc snickered.

"Just open your receiver and hold, wise guy."

Alex picked up her camera and turned the top function knob to a modified "burst" icon, then pressed the shutter button and held it. The SLR started transmitting her audio file in an uplink to Linc via her ear comm, which squealed in her ear and made her wince. But it was a burst transmission, and the entire half hour of audio surveillance uploaded in less than twenty seconds. Then a completion signal beeped.

"You got that, sport?" Alex said.

"Got it," Linc said. "It's in Russian I think."

"Really? And here I thought they'd be speaking Sanskrit. Well, use Google Translate, genius."

Linc laughed. "I think we can do a bit better than that."

Alex waited for a while as she rummaged through the Russian snacks on her table and wished she'd packed some Snickers. Then Linc came back on the line.

"Okay," he said. "This is a digital voice translation, so you'll only hear one type of voice for both players."

"I'll figure it out," Alex said.

"Running," Linc said.

Alex listened. For the first minutes there wasn't much to speak of—mostly rustling, some small talk, and what sounded like cups on saucers and a cigarette lighter flaring up. Then a full conversation came on, and her eyes widened as the drama progressed, until it finally ended with the sound of someone retching and a small commotion inside the suite.

"Holy moly," she said to Linc. "Did you hear all that?"

"Yes, and not only me. Your DNA donor and his partner heard it too."

Alex rolled her eyes. "What's my venerable ancestor saying?" she asked, meaning her dad.

"He didn't say anything to me, only to Conley. 'Fly faster.'"

"Does he understand the stakes here, Linc?" Alex prodded. "This isn't about getting his baby home to Mama. We're talking satellites, nuclear warheads, extortion, blackmail and a hostage."

"I believe he does," Linc said drily, "and he just passed me a note to prove it." Alex heard paper rustling, and then Linc went on. "It says, 'tell Alex to just stay in her berth and hunker down.'"

"Right," she scoffed. "Just like *he* would."

"He's serious, Alex ..." Linc started to say.

But Alex pulled out her ear comm, switched it off, kicked off her sneakers, re-donned her boots and tucked her knife firmly in place. She chewed down half a Russian fruit bar, washed it down with mineral water, then didn't stay in her berth and certainly didn't hunker down.

CHAPTER FIVE

Alexander "Sasha" Dubkin was nearing the glorious day of his retirement. Thirty years aboard rattling old trains was enough, and he was looking forward to that tiny cottage beside a St. Petersburg lake, lazy days fishing from his battered old skiff, and playing with his grandchildren. His legs were like those of a veteran boatswain—they would last for years, until even his progeny were too old to play.

Now he stood on those sinewy legs, encased in a full-body set of button-up long underwear, inside the tiny berth that had served as his cabin for too many years. A pot of fresh tea boiled on a rusty electrical hot plate and he held a long pencil in his stubby fingers, "conducting" a passage from Igor Stravinsky's *The Rite of Spring* as it crackled from an old plug-in radio.

More and more these days, he craved the nights when he was off duty, and the trains fell silent to no more than snores. Someday soon, he would no longer have to pose the request that he'd uttered a million times: "Ticket, please."

A soft knock on his cabin door stopped his pencil baton in mid-motion. He wondered if it was the radio's aberration, but then it came again. He rolled his eyes, raised his bushy eyebrows, switched off the radio, turned the key and slid the door open a crack, fully prepared to read whoever was disturbing him the riot act.

The large brown eyes of that pretty, pixie-faced American girl blinked at him. "Sasha, may I speak with you a moment?" she asked.

He frowned. "It is very late, Miss Alex."

"Just for a minute. It truly is important. Please?"

Sasha lowered his head and remembered that he had decided some hours ago that he liked the girl. She seemed kind and her youthful energy was infectious. Besides, he wasn't retired yet, and a train conductor's job was not done until all passengers were safely off at their destination. He closed the door, muttered some complaint noises even he didn't understand, threw on a woolen robe, and pulled the door open again.

Alex smiled sympathetically as well as thankfully, slipped inside, and slid it closed behind her. She looked around his dreary berth.

"This looks … comfy," she said.

"False flattery is an American trait," Sasha scoffed. "You should try being more Russian. Say what you mean."

"Okay," Alex said as she looked around more carefully. "I could live here for maybe a week and then I'd go crazy."

"Much better." Sasha gestured at a gnarled old chair with a worn lime seat. "Tea, Miss Alex?"

"Yes, thank you." Alex sat. She hated tea.

Sasha poured two cups from his steaming pot, handed one to Alex, and sat down facing her on the edge of his too-slim bed. "And so, how can I help you? Is your cabin not comfortable?"

Alex held her teacup, but she didn't sip. "Sasha, I have to confess something. Abroad, I am a photographer, as I told you. But at home, I am sort of a detective."

Sasha smirked and cocked his thick-haired head. "You are far too young to be a detective."

"Are you sure?" Alex posed. "Were the Russian female snipers who fought at Stalingrad too young?"

Sasha frowned and waved his stubby finger at her. "As I have said before, you are also far too smart, Miss Alex. So, if what you say is true …"

Alex took out her iPhone and showed Sasha the picture of Dmitry Kozlov. "Do you know this man, Sasha?"

He looked at the photo. "No, but he is aboard this train, and he looks very much like …" Sasha paused, unable to remember the name.

"Yes, he does," Alex responded, coming to his rescue. "He is Dmitry Kozlov, the aerospace scientist."

Sasha pulled his head back and touched the ends of his bushy mustache. "The famous one?"

"Not famous enough for you to remember his name, but yes. And he is aboard this train with a group of Serbian mercenaries who are holding him hostage."

Sasha stared at her for a second, and Alex could see many emotions flitting across his face, finishing up with self-preservation.

"Nonsense, my girl!" he chuckled dismissively, then took a long, covering sip of black tea before finally putting the cup down, having decided on a weak follow-up. "You have been reading too much American fiction. Try some Chekhov."

Alex wasn't sure why the gent was suggesting she search out the books of Star Trek's helmsman, but she didn't have time to find out he was referring to a great Russian writer. Instead, she reached across the small space, and gripped his knee with conviction and urgency.

"It's true, Sasha. I have had it confirmed. Believe me, I wouldn't make this up for any reason."

He looked down at her hand, then back up to her face. "Then perhaps we should consult with Boris," he said cautiously, referring to the onboard policeman.

"I considered that, but any intervention could place Kozlov in further danger. And there are seven of them and only one Boris. I also believe these people had something to do with the death of that passenger, Yankovski."

Sasha leaned back, his expression conflicted, and, finally, overwhelmed. "This will all be something for the proper authorities, Miss Alex. I shall personally summon them when we arrive at Irkutsk."

"We may not arrive at Irkutsk, Sasha."

Now the old Stalinite looked alarmed. "What do you mean?"

"Sasha, these men are plotting something that will happen aboard this train. They have some equipment hidden somewhere. Could there be such a secret compartment in one of the cars?"

"Well …" Sasha hesitated. He wanted no part of this intrigue, and his only desire was to get rid of this girl and go to sleep. "There are some cargo compartments aboard that can be rented. They are locked and can only be entered by the customers."

"Only by the customers, Sasha?"

"Well, and by me, of course."

"Show me, please."

Once more Alex witnessed the argument going on behind the conductor's eyes. But, finally, she saw that he recognized the possible danger etched into the faces of those Serbians.

"*Blyat*," Sasha muttered in Russian, pressed his hands to his knees, and got up. He pulled a small scrolled poster from a cardboard tube tucked next to his bed, and unfurled it. It was a schematic diagram of the Trans-Siberian, detailing all the cars' layouts from a birds-eye view. He stretched the scroll out on his bed coverlet as Alex got up and looked down at it.

"You see?" he said. "Here, up front near the locomotive, there is a cargo compartment with four large lockers. They were berths before being converted, but I assure you that nothing of danger is in there."

"How do you know, Sasha?"

The conductor puffed out his chest. "Alex, I am much like the captain of a ship ..."

"Once you rent someone a locker, do you see everything that goes in there?"

"Well, not always. But passengers are most often shipping their personal effects. Sometimes they are moving, with clothing and suitcases and dishware."

With that, Alex knelt on both knees and laced her fingers together on the edge of Sasha's bed. She looked up at him with such sincerity that he was taken aback.

"Sasha," she said. "Are you a patriot?"

"Of course. I am a devoted child of Mother Russia!"

"Well, your mother is in grave danger, Sasha. Perhaps mortal danger. If you don't believe me, go have a look at Yankovski's cold corpse."

Sasha said nothing, but his expression turned very grave, and his sharp old eyes began to melt in surrender.

"Take me to these compartments, Sasha," Alex said. "If I am wrong, you can laugh at me afterwards." She looked over at his ancient radio. "And I'll buy you a brand new stereo, battery powered, and a whole set of all the classics, loaded on an iPod that plugs right in. I'll even look up the works of ensign Chekov."

"Anton Chekov," Sasha said. But then he got up, shrugged off his robe, pulled his uniform pants from a hook and started dressing.

"I knew you were going to be trouble the first time I saw you," he said.

Alex grinned. "That's what my father always says."

* * * *

It was well past midnight, and except for the rolling pitch of its cars and the constant clacks of its old iron wheels, the train was quiet. Only a few passengers moved through the corridors, most of whom trudged to the toilets in slippers. The dining cars were empty.

Alex followed Sasha as he made his way forward, noting his bow-legged, but steady, gait, and she felt an affinity for the kind old Russian. She had never known her grandfathers, and decided that such nurturing souls reached across nationalities, borders and politics.

Her stomach only tensed as they passed through the car where Kreesat and his crew occupied their two suites, but he'd posted no guard and the doors were closed. A few minutes later they had negotiated all of the passenger cars, arrived at a coupling, and faced a locked iron door with no window. Sasha produced a collection of skeleton keys on a large brass ring.

"It is foolishness," he muttered as the wind stream coursed through the coupling's cracked flex shields.

"I don't mind being proved a fool," Alex said.

"It is because you are young," Sasha said as he cranked the key. "The taste grows bitter as one gets older." He pulled the heavy door open and disappeared into utter blackness.

Alex followed, squinting hard but seeing absolutely nothing, until Sasha flicked on the battery-powered hurricane lantern he'd brought along. The weak bulb flickered, throwing pale yellow shadows along a car corridor stripped of any comforts—no carpeting or drapes on the windows. The berths on the right hadn't been painted for years, and the rusty doors all had heavy padlocks hanging from hasps. She pulled the car's entrance door closed behind her.

"We do not care very much for this space," Sasha said with a hint of embarrassment.

"I can see that," Alex said, though she wasn't sure if Sasha meant that the train crew didn't like the cargo car, or that they didn't bother to dust.

Sasha waved at the cargo berths. "Where do you wish to begin, Miss Alex?"

"At the beginning, please."

He flipped through his massive key ring, until he found an additional set of padlock keys with numbers that matched their locks. He worked the first berth's lock open, hung the heavy padlock from his leather belt, slid the door aside, and raised his lantern. Alex, considerably taller than Sasha, stuck her face over his shoulder and peered inside. She saw nothing more than a pile of suitcases and steamer trunks.

"May I open one of those, Sasha?" she asked.

"No, but I may if you wish."

"Please."

Sasha walked into the berth, flipped the hasp of one thick wooden trunk and opened the lid. It was packed with books, and he looked up at Alex and snorted, "Unless your criminals are violent librarians, I think we are done with this one."

Alex agreed and they locked up and moved to the next berth. She had hope as the light from the hurricane lantern gleamed off of large metal boxes, but they turned out to be filing cabinets filled with legal briefs.

"There is an attorney on board with his family," Sasha said. "It appears he has had his fill of Siberian courts and is moving to Moscow. Would you like to read his files, Miss Alex?"

"I don't read Russian."

"Well, I could leave you here anyway. Maybe you'd learn."

Alex put her fists to her hips and dipped her forehead. "Very funny, Sasha. Can we move on?"

"As you wish."

As they opened the third cargo berth, both of them gasped and jumped back. In the middle of the berth between a neat pile of suitcases and household goods packed in cardboard boxes, was a standing birdcage with a huge white cockatoo inside that started flapping and screaming.

"Jesus!" Alex touched her thumping heart, while Sasha recovered the huge key ring he'd dropped on the floor.

"Some people have pets," he said. "They cannot be with them in the cars."

"At least it wasn't a lion."

Sasha locked the berth, looked at his pocket watch and then up at Alex from under his wild eyebrows. "I think we have seen enough. Nothing is here, Miss Alex."

"But there's only one more, Sasha."

"Oh, all right," he huffed as he walked to the last one. "But you are far too inquisitive. Or how do they say it in English?" He touched his bulbous veiny nose.

"Nosy."

"Yes! If you were my granddaughter …"

"I'd be a very fortunate girl."

"You do not need to flatter me, Alex," he admonished as he opened the last lock.

"I meant it."

Sasha slid the door open, raised his lantern, and froze.

"*Oh my God*," Alex blurted in a hoarse whisper.

Both of them stood in the doorway, mouths agape. This cargo compartment was devoid of any household or business goods. To the left against the forward wall of the train car was a slim metal table with a tucked-under chair, and on top of the table sat a sophisticated single sideband radio set, its power cord plugged into a black extension cord that snaked off somewhere.

Across from that, against the right-hand bulkhead, was a black tower of much more complex communications equipment, topped by a wire-array antenna that looked somewhat like a large, black praying mantis. This multi-comm module was not plugged into the train's juice either, but instead attached to some sort of gasoline generator sitting on the floor, which in turn was encased in a soundproof "blimp" and was chugging out electricity almost silently. The power lights on the comm tower flickered and blinked in a steady rhythm.

And sitting in the middle of the berth between these two sections of digital wares, on a hard-backed steel chair, was a young blond woman about thirty years old. She was wearing a stained green blouse and a business-like gray skirt, no shoes. Her trunk was tied to the chair back with coils of rough hemp, her arms cranked behind her, and her ankles were trussed to the chair legs. A long filthy silk scarf was tied horizontally around her head, its soggy twists parting her pale lips like a horse bit. Her green eyes were gleaming and wild and her chest heaved.

"What *is* this?!" Sasha exclaimed in rage and made to jump to the woman's rescue, but Alex gripped his arm and yanked him back.

"Wait, Sasha," she ordered, and she took the lantern from his clenched fist and lowered the light, examining the space for some kind of trip wire. Seeing nothing, she released him and he sprang forward. He quickly untied the woman's gag and threw it away as he pulled a handkerchief from his pocket and gently wiped her drooling mouth and saliva-soaked chin.

"My poor dear," he said in Russian. "What in heaven's name happened to you?"

But the woman couldn't speak. Alex looked around and spotted a water bottle on the floor near the right-hand wall, next to a bowl of some sort of gruel and a pail for human waste. Yet none of those items could be of use to a bound hostage, unless she were regularly visited by her captors. She picked up the water bottle and gently sluiced some into the woman's lips. Then she finger brushed her wild blond hair back from her face and bent to talk to her, but Sasha was very agitated and broke in first.

"Who are you?" he asked in Russian.

"You are Svetlana Kozlov, aren't you?" Alex said to her in English.

"*Da*," the woman whispered, and then added in English, "I am Svetlana."

"She is Svetlana Kozlov!" Sasha said to Alex.

"I *know*, Sasha," Alex said. "She just said it in English."

"You are the daughter of the famous physicist!" Sasha said to Svetlana in Russian. "I read the story, but the newspapers all said you died."

"She's the daughter of Dmitry Kozlov," Alex said to Sasha in English.

"I know that!" he repeated. "I read and speak Russian well!" Then Sasha jumped to the back of Svetlana's chair and made to untie her wrists, but Alex reached out, squeezed his shoulder, and looked in his furious eyes.

"No, Sasha. Not yet." She knelt and placed her hands on Svetlana's trembling thighs and looked at her tortured pale face. "Svetlana, my name is Alex. I am here to help you. Do you understand me?"

"Yes," Svetlana said.

"*We* are here to help you," Sasha corrected.

"Yes, we." Alex looked up at him over Svetlana's shoulder. "Do you believe me now, Sasha?"

"Yes, yes!"

Alex turned her attention back to the woman. "How did you get here?"

"Serbians," Svetlana whispered in a croak. "Six terrible men and one young female."

Sasha, unable as yet to free the woman, took to gently petting her hair. "But how did they bring you in here, my poor dear?"

"On board as a regular passenger with a ticket," Alex guessed. "And then in here, probably at gunpoint. Is that right?"

Svetlana shuddered with a sob. "Please let me go," she begged.

"We will," Alex said. "But we can't just yet."

"Why?" Tears welled in Svetlana's eyes and rolled down her quivering cheeks.

"Why not?" Sasha demanded.

Alex ignored him. "Listen to me, Svetlana. Your father is also on this train, and he is in grave danger, just like you."

"*Nyet*. Oh no ..."

"Yes." Alex held the woman's shocked gaze. "And you can imagine what these people want from him, can't you?"

"He is an important scientist." Svetlana glanced around at the communications gear. "A brilliant man."

"Yes." Alex touched her chin to bring her focus back. "And when he thought you were dead, he was broken. But now he knows you are alive somewhere, though he does not know you are on this train. Only Sasha and I know that, and these Serbs have no idea that we know. They are planning to force your father to do something terrible. We cannot give them any warning. Do you understand?"

Then the woman began to comprehend, as did Sasha, though he was shaking his old head behind Svetlana and murmuring keening sounds. Svetlana slumped as she stared at Alex.

"I must stay here, like this, for now."

"Yes," Alex said. "Just for now."

Alex turned to search for the sodden gag where Sasha had thrown it to the floor. The last thing she wanted to do was to leave this woman alone in her terror, but if she freed her now and the Serbians discovered her gone, they might act out in ways that could be murderous to everyone on board the train.

She stopped searching for the rag as her eyes fixed on something attached to one leg of the metal table on the left. It was a small disk, the shape and thickness of a bottle cap, with a gleaming glass orb in the center. Her heart started hammering as she turned her head to the comm tower over on the right, where she spotted a similar module affixed to one upright stanchion of the power rack. The two "bottle caps" were directly in line with each other, positioned about six inches in front of Svetlana's ankles. Alex was kneeling right there, between them.

It was an electric eye—a digital tripwire. At that very moment, a receiver alarm was probably beeping in Maxim Kreesat's cell phone. She reached out, snatched up Svetlana's gag and got up.

"Sasha, where is Boris?" she asked him.

"The policeman? He is probably asleep, and drunk."

"Go get him."

"But why?"

"*Now* Sasha! I will stay here with Svetlana. Go!"

He cursed in a string of Russian mumbles and made for the door. Then he turned back and offered Alex the lantern.

"No, take it with you. And padlock the door again after you leave."

He complied, and the door slid home and the cargo berth was plunged into blackness.

Alex worked her way behind Svetlana's chair in the dark, and gently retied the gag in her mouth. Then she leaned down and whispered in her ear. "Just sit very still and act exactly like you have before, okay?"

Svetlana nodded, although Alex could smell the rank sweat and adrenaline fear rising from the poor woman's skin. She worked her way in the dark to the near right corner of the berth, in front of the comm tower rack and just behind the door. Then she whispered once more in the dark.

"Don't be afraid," she said, for both their benefits. "I am a very capable girl."

CHAPTER SIX

The doorway to Maxim Kreesat's suite was filled with the enormous frame of Vlado Hislak, formerly the sergeant major of the Shadows—and a very capable man. Hislak gripped the door frame with his ham hock hands, and thrust his grizzly-sized head and wild beard inside, as if he were a jump master checking the drop zone from the door of a paratroop transport.

"Yes, Major?" He looked down at Kreesat, who was large himself, but few men were as massive as Hislak.

The Ghost showed Hislak his smart phone and the small orange icon blinking in the upper right corner of the screen. "Something has set off the digital tripwire, Vlado," Kreesat said. "Go check on it."

"Yes, sir," Hislak said with a voice that sounded like a dump truck engine. He glanced toward the sleeping compartment, and tipped his red beard up at Amina. She stood there, arms folded, keeping watch over the reclining form of Dmitry Kozlov, who lay under a thin blanket—a cold wash cloth soothing his eyes. Amina tipped her cleft chin back up at Hislak, then unsnapped a large key ring from her belt and flung it across the space. Hislak caught it like a Frisbee.

"The odd-looking key opens the main door of the cargo car," Kreesat said to Hislak. "The rest are numbered accordingly, but you should only need the fourth one. Call me as soon as you see that she is exactly where we left her."

"Yes, sir." Hislak shoved the keys in the pocket of his sheepskin vest.

"Are you armed, Vlado?" Kreesat asked.

"Only with my blade. Do you think I need more than that?"

"You never have before."

Hislak grinned, an expression reminiscent of a bearded Jack-O-Lantern, then slid the door closed with a slam that rattled the berth window.

He started off for the forward sections of the train. For a man of his size he moved with a certain grace, although some might have described his gait as a thundering stagger that appeared to be fueled by vodka. He wore a pair of Cossack boots over thick woolen trousers, with an open neck flannel shirt revealing a hedgerow of chest curls. His sheepskin vest completed the throwback image of a villain from *Rasputin the Mad Monk*.

Vlado Hislak was happiest when tasked with some sort of mission, and his horse-like strides matched his enthusiasm. In just three minutes he had reached the door of the cargo car, nearly yanked it off its steel hinges, and was deep inside the long swaying box, with a black Maglite flashlight wedged into the right side of his mouth—between his broken teeth and steel fillings. He used the beam to find the correct padlock key, and opened the lock on cargo berth Number Four.

He hung the heavy padlock from his trouser pocket, grabbed the door handle and wrenched it to the left, where it squealed along its tracks before banging open hard. The berth was completely dark inside.

Vlado stepped in, slid the door closed behind him—just in case some other passenger decided to come fiddle with his or her housewares—and reached up to twist the Maglite's head into high-beam. And there was the woman, right in front of him, trussed to her chair and gagged—exactly as they'd left her after her last piss and feeding four hours before.

Vlado shrugged. "*Pacovi*," he mumbled in Serbian, deciding that scurrying rats had no doubt triggered the major's digital tripwire. But then he looked again at the scientist's daughter. Before this, whenever they came to attend to her, her head had been hanging down as if she were sleeping. This time, however, she was staring directly at him, her eyes looked somewhat wild, and she appeared to be breathing very quickly. He cocked his massive head to the right as he placed his melon size fists to his hips and wondered …

The top of Alex's right foot whipped through the air at ninety miles per hour in a flashing roundhouse that impacted perfectly with the lens of Hislak's Maglite. And given that the steel flashlight was tucked in his teeth like a six-inch long toothpick, the impact speared it directly back into his throat.

His eyes flew open in shock and his brain registered nothing but the searing agony of metal crushing his glottis. He staggered backward and slammed into the berth door as his hands flew up to his throat.

But almost immediately came a new sensation, as Alex stomped down on the floor with her right foot that she'd just used as a flying sledgehammer, and whipped her body around in a spinning back kick that buried her heel into Vlado's gonads—and he wasn't wearing a protective cup.

As the huge man's hands flipped down from his throat and scrambled for his wounded groin, Alex had the fleeting thought that her dad was right about learning all the very best techniques of various martial arts and plucking from that menu whatever the occasion warranted—in this case Kyokushin Karate.

And then, as the Serbian giant dropped to his knees and the flashlight buried in his mouth still flicked enough light around the berth so that she could see, Alex spotted the heavy padlock still swaying from his trouser pocket.

This next move's not from any dojo I've ever seen, she thought as she snatched up the heavy lock by its gleaming "U," whipped it over her head like a lasso, and rang the steel casing off Hislak's skull right where his bushy red eyebrows met. His eyes rolled back, showing nothing but white, and he crashed facedown on the floor.

That last blow had caused him to retch out the flashlight. Alex picked it up and frowned as she wiped the slime off on her jeans and scanned him to be certain he was really out. She kicked him once in the temple just to make sure, but his head only lolled like a rag doll's. Then she turned the light on Svetlana to check that she was still all right, and found the Russian woman slowly shaking her still gagged head in wonder at what she'd just witnessed. Alex smiled.

"The bigger they are ..."

She didn't bother to finish.

* * * *

When Vlado failed to signal Kreesat that all was well with the Kozlov woman—and also failed to return—the Ghost realized that the game had changed. Control was something he cherished above all other operational advantages, and he no longer had it.

Whatever had triggered his digital tripwire, it was clearly no mouse, cockroach, or moth. And given Vlado's size and strength, the opposition was a force to be reckoned with, and could well be multiple unknown persons.

Still, he reasoned, Vlado Hislak wasn't the brightest bulb in the box. He might have forgotten to charge his cell phone or been distracted by some seductive snack in a dining car. Perhaps all was still well up forward. Kreesat doubted that was the case, but there was only one way to find out.

At precisely the half hour mark after Hislak had departed from the berth, Kreesat rose from his couch, checked the Zastava CZ99 9mm pistol tucked in his leather shoulder holster, and called out to Amina as he pulled on his black leather jacket.

"I am going up to the cargo car to see what happened with Vlado. Stay here and keep watch over our guest."

"Yes, sir," Amina called back from the sleeping compartment. "Are you going alone?"

"No. I'll take Karl with me. Are you armed?"

"I have my knife," she said.

"Arm yourself better," Kreesat ordered. "And prepare for combat. Vlado should have returned by now."

"I will," she said. Kreesat heard her unzipping her Kevlar lined backpack where she secreted her more serious tools of the trade.

Kreesat stepped into the corridor and looked around before moving to the adjoining berth. He summoned Karl, a short ex-commando with ginger hair who resembled a fire plug. Karl, who whenever on leave from special forces, had engaged in cage fighting as a hobby, asked no questions of his commander, and simply followed along. Kreesat didn't bother to ask if Karl was armed—he always carried at least one handgun and two knives.

In short order, they reached the coupling to the cargo car. Finding the steel entrance door unlocked, Kreesat drew his CZ99, as well as a powerful tactical Streamlight, and Karl followed suit, gripping a heavy .45 caliber PPZ. They rushed the entrance simultaneously, then split from each other to both flanks, then crouched, ready to fire.

But nothing threatened them inside the rocking, dusty car. Kreesat then moved carefully forward, shining his beam to inspect every cargo berth lock—until he found the last door slightly ajar, the padlock gone from its hasp.

He wrenched the berth door open on its rails. Both men braced the open doorway, and stared. Svetlana Kozlov was gone from her chair. In her place sat Vlado Hislak, with the sodden scarf that had been used to gag the Russian journalist stuffed in his drooling mouth. His hands were tied behind his back, his Cossack boots gone, and his beefy ankles were roped together below the chair seat. But the chair wasn't resting fully on the floor.

It was tilted precariously backward, and the only thing supporting Vlado's girth was his own slim black flashlight, which had somehow been jammed as a support between the train car floor and the bottom of one front chair leg. From the slat ceiling above, and an ancient rusty cargo hook, a taut length of hemp led down to Vlado's bulging neck. It was knotted tightly under his beard, which glistened with his saliva.

Although Vlado's bear brown eyes were wide, he was barely breathing or moving. All it would take was a cough or even a wheeze to dislodge the flashlight brace, and Vlado would've choked to death after several agonizing minutes.

Kreesat lowered his gun, and regarded his sergeant major like some fascinating insect pinned to a display box. He was furious, but intensely curious as well. How the hell had anyone been able to haul this monster into that chair? And then he spotted the trickle of blood crawling down Hislak's flannel shirt from directly under his beard.

Ah, that was it. He had first been knocked silly—the evidence being a swollen egg in the middle of his forehead. Then he'd been trussed, in such a way that he could still maneuver his own body. Then, the point of a knife had been twisted up into his throat, with the implications clear: "Get yourself into this chair, or die right here."

"Should I cut him down, Major?" Karl asked Kreesat as he regarded his helpless comrade.

"Yes, but carefully." Kreesat pulled out his smart phone, and tapped on Amina's icon.

"Yes, sir?" she answered.

"It was a rat after all," Kreesat said. "But a large one, and clever. Our guest is gone."

"*Govno*," Amina grunted, using the Serbian's favorite five-letter word meaning excrement.

"No matter. Bring me Kozlov, quickly. And feel free to break his arm if he resists. I only need his brain."

CHAPTER SEVEN

Dmitry Kozlov's fingers trembled as he sat at the slim metal table inside cargo berth Number Four.

His hands were poised above a Bluetooth keyboard that Kreesat had pulled from a metal drawer, and directly in front of him, atop the single side band transceiver, a glowing computer monitor displayed a spider web of satellite tracks—twisting and criss-crossing above a slowly spinning image of the globe.

Work lights glowed from above, where Karl had clipped them to the same rusty cargo hook that had nearly been the end of Vlado—their corkscrew wires running down to the blimp-encased generator that droned along, tainting the space with nauseating fumes.

Over in the right corner before the complex comm tower, Vlado Hislak sat in the same steel chair as before, but now he was un-trussed and rather subdued. He leaned his head back and held a large plastic bag of ice to his pounding forehead—a salve that Amina had kindly fetched from one of the dining cars.

Karl, his .45 PPZ still gripped in his hand, stood to the right of Kozlov's chair, watching the old scientist's every move. The trembling ancient could hardly be much of a threat, and yet, someone had taken down Vlado—a phenomenon that no one had ever seen before, so all bets were off.

Kreesat, arms folded, stood to the left of Kozlov's position, maintaining his full composure in tones of "advice and consent." He very much wanted to know who had freed the scientist's daughter and beaten his sergeant major, but the giant was clearly concussed and taking some time to recover.

No rush. Kreesat had Kozlov, the disks, and the old man's terror in the palm of his hand.

"Are the disks reading well?" Kreesat asked Kozlov.

The old man glanced at the blinking multiple disk trays just to the right of the monitor. "Yes, they are functional."

"Good. Then you may go ahead and produce an uplink to Laika II."

Kozlov looked up at Kreesat, and raised a palm toward the comm tower to his right. "That is only a satcom antenna, Mr. Kreesat. As I explained to you before, we would need specialized equipment to do this. The range is far beyond what …"

"There is a microwave dish mounted on the roof of this car, Doctor." Kreesat looked at Karl, who smiled. "My men actually assembled it up there while the train was in motion. They are quite good with their hands."

Kozlov's bony shoulders slumped. "I see."

"Talk to your satellite, Doctor. And no more stalling. Tell me its current location."

Kozlov pointed a jittery old finger at the monitor. "It is there, above Newfoundland."

"Good. Now fire its thrusters, take it out of orbit, and re-task it for a track over Washington, D.C. Do I need to give you the coordinates? Or do you think you can figure that out yourself?"

"Of course I can," Kozlov mumbled as he began to tap the keyboard. Behind him, on the comm tower, a row of green lights began oscillating somewhat like a small Christmas tree, and shortly thereafter one of the satellite icons on the monitor began glowing in kind, with lime-colored pulses. "You realize, Mr. Kreesat," Kozlov said, "that the Americans will be able to trace the origin of this transmission."

"Actually, they won't. It is masked. Thanks to the Russian government, my team is also well-versed in encryption codes and fills."

After another minute, Kozlov sat back in his chair and dropped his hands to his sides. "There, it has turned and is proceeding south. What do you wish me to do now?"

"Nothing," Kreesat said as he turned to Karl. "Hand me that satphone."

Karl pulled a satphone from a charger atop the comm tower and handed it over to his commander. Kreesat powered it up and dialed a U.S. telephone number.

"This is the White House," a female voice answered. "Good morning and how can we help you today?"

"Good morning!" Kreesat said brightly. "You can help me by giving me the National Security Advisor."

"Who may I ask is calling, sir?"

"Major Maxim Kreesat, formerly Serbian special forces. It is a matter of some urgency."

"One moment, please."

Kreesat waited, and then a more officious female voice came on the line.

"Lara Longren, here. How can I help you, Major Kreesat?"

"Good morning, Ms. Longren. What is your position, please?"

"Deputy NSA to General Socroft."

"Very good," Kreesat said, and since he was bent on savoring the next part, he took a moment to light up a Sobranie. "Ms. Longren, I am going to dispense with the niceties and get right to the point. I am a terrorist."

"Excuse me?" The Deputy National Security Advisor tried to suppress a laugh.

Kreesat smiled himself. "Yes, I know it is not the normal, formal way of introduction. However, I used to be a government servant like yourself, but I discovered that the pay and appreciation were minimal. Today, I have control of a Russian nuclear launch platform disguised as a communications satellite—its NATO moniker is Laika II. I also happen to be holding its developer, Doctor Dmitry Kozlov, as my hostage, along with the satellite operational codes and frequencies. Are you following me so far, Ms. Longren?"

"Yes. I am transcribing every word."

"That seems redundant, since you record all incoming calls. But no matter. Rather than trying to convince you of the veracity of my claims, I would like you to call the Pentagon and ask them for a real-time track of Laika II, via the National Reconnaissance Office. You will find that I have taken Laika II off of its longitudinal track above Newfoundland—which happens to be minus five seven point six six oh four three six four, decimal degrees—and have repositioned it to a latitudinal track of plus three eight point nine zero seven one nine two three, decimal degrees, which splices Washington, D.C. It is currently moving south at an altitude of one hundred and twenty-three miles, and a speed of six thousand meters per second, as it is no longer geosynchronous." Kreesat waited for Longren's response, but all he heard was her breathing. "Ms. Longren?"

"Yes, Major," she said. "I'm still here. What do you want?"

"We'll discuss that in half an hour when I call back, Ms. Longren. I imagine that it will take half of that time simply to convince the NRO that this isn't some sort of April Fools joke, even though spring has long passed. Oh, and by the way, please emphasize that Laika II is a Trojan horse. It is actually a MIRV platform with five nuclear warheads aboard. You might want to also advise Treasury that they'll soon be moving large sums of money."

Kreesat tapped the satphone keypad, ending the call, and then he also powered the transceiver off—no sense in tempting a missile strike that might ride down the waves of his transmissions and spoil everyone's night. He turned to Karl and pointed at Kozlov's back.

"Watch him, Karl. If he touches anything without permission, smash his fingers. And keep an eye on Vlado here as well …"

"It was a girl," Vlado croaked from under his ice bag.

"Excuse me?" Kreesat said as he turned.

"A girl. She hit me with something, maybe a sledge hammer, and then she used the lock on my face. That was when I saw her. A girl, slim, strong, short brown hair."

"A *girl*?" Kreesat almost laughed. "Well, Vlado, if that's true, when we find her I'll let you dismember her."

"Yes, thank you, Major."

"My pleasure." Kreesat pulled out his smart phone again, tapped a contact icon and called another of his men back at their onboard headquarters suite.

"*Da, majore*," a heavy voice answered.

"Bojan, go find the train's chief conductor, as well as the onboard policeman, and escort them up here to the cargo car. But wait with them in the coupling and call me. Clear?"

"Yes, Major."

Kreesat cocked his head at Amina, and they left the berth together, sliding the door closed behind them. Kreesat had the ring of keys in his hand. He dropped his Sobranie on the floor and cranked it out with a boot as he walked to the first cargo berth, opened the lock, and swept Amina inside with a gracious hand.

She pulled a small chemlight from her pocket and bent it in half until it glowed green, then set it down on a suitcase while she backed up and hiked herself up onto the large crate of books that Sasha and Alex had inspected before. She smiled at Kreesat as she reached down and pulled off her turtleneck. He smiled back, opened his belt buckle and unzipped his leather pants.

"Is it going to be enough?" Amina asked as she raised her muscled buttocks and stripped her bobsledder's spandex down off her thighs.

"It's never enough," Kreesat said. "But half an hour is all we have."

Amina laughed. "I meant the money."

"Ah, I think so, yes. Five hundred million from the Americans, and then the equivalent amount from the Russians." He reached down and dragged her spandex off over her running shoes as she pulled her sports bra off over her blond head. "You can buy the silence of an entire African village with much, much less."

"Have you picked one out already?" She leaned forward and gripped his flesh in her fist, licking her lips as she pulled him toward her.

"Yes." He shuffled forward with his leathers crumpled about his boots, and he reached down for her ankles and lifted them up, high and wide. "It's on the shores of an enormous lake in Ethiopia, Lake Tana. Maybe we'll become pirates there."

"We already are," she said, and then she raised a finger. "Take your pistol out, Major. It always bruises my ribs."

Kreesat pulled his CZ from his holster and laid it down somewhere. Then he gripped her by the hair, and she gripped his in turn, and they slammed into each other.

* * * *

Twenty minutes later—a full fifteen minutes more than Kreesat and Amina needed to sate their lust—Sasha and Boris stood inside the cargo car's coupling, waiting to be told why they'd been summoned in the middle of the night.

Sasha, of course, already knew that he'd fallen upon a mortally dangerous venture of some sort, and although he wanted nothing to do with it, there was no erasing what he had already seen. After Alex had ordered him to go fetch the policeman, he and Boris had only made it halfway back to the cargo car when she and that poor pathetic Svetlana woman had come rocketing toward them. Alex had stopped and gripped his shoulders and whispered in a rush, "I'm taking her and hiding her somewhere, Sasha. Don't give us up!"

So he and Boris had then turned around and wandered back to their separate quarters. But half an hour later, they'd both been gathered up by this tall, blond, pony-tailed Serb who called himself Bojan. That, in itself, was not a good sign, as Sasha knew that, in Serbian, the name meant "warrior."

And Boris, fairly much dazed and confused, was not going to be of much help. The old cops assigned to the Trans-Siberian were on the cusp of retirement and unarmed, which made them about as effective as a shopping mall security guard.

The two stood in the vibrating coupling, with that Bojan character towering over them from behind. After a few minutes, the door to the cargo car opened and the large commanding one that Sasha had seen with the old scientist, smiled down at them, and it was not a smile of warmth and welcome.

"What is your name, conductor?" Kreesat asked.

"Alexander Dubkin. What is yours, sir?"

"Kreesat. And you, policeman?"

"Boris Spelski."

"Sounds vaguely Polish," Kreesat said.

"Do you have a complaint about something on this train?" Boris asked in his official policeman's tone.

Kreesat nodded. "I do. I have lost a valuable piece of property, stolen by one of your female passengers."

"You may file a complaint and I shall investigate," Boris said as he pulled a small notebook and a pen from his uniform pocket.

"I have no patience for *apparatchik* bureaucracy," Kreesat said as he reached down and snatched Sasha's large key ring from the elder man's belt. He handed it over Sasha's shoulder to Bojan and cocked his head at the coupling's boarding door. "It is stuffy in here, Bojan. Give us some air."

The large blond Serb smiled, rattled through some keys until he found a large steel skeleton, turned it in the lock and slid the door open. The cold night air rushed in and thundered through the coupling chamber. Kreesat had to raise his voice.

"Boris, I want you to collect the passports of all female passengers on this train and bring them to me."

Boris puffed up his chest. "I cannot do that, nor will I, sir."

Kreesat reached out with his left hand, gripped Boris's uniform lapels and backed him over to the open door ledge. The policeman's eyes bugged white and his mouth opened, but he was given no chance to change his mind as Kreesat drew his CZ99 and shot him point blank in the chest. Then there was nothing but the open doorway. Only Sasha remained, his knees trembling like those of a newborn foal.

"And then there was one," Kreesat said as the wind swept a curl of smoke from his gun barrel. "I trust you will be more cooperative, Mr. Dubkin. If not, you can expect every passenger on this train to follow in Boris's footsteps."

Sasha said nothing.

"All the passports, please. And this is a good time to do it, as the passengers will be either sleeping or in their berths or seats. Bojan here will accompany you. There should also be a ticket stub displayed at every passenger's position, yes?"

"Yes," Sasha croaked.

"Good. So, if anyone is missing, I am sure you will note that and advise me. Oh, and bring me the entire passenger list as well. You have one hour."

"I … I cannot do all of this so quickly," Sasha protested. "We are nearing Irkutsk and many people will shortly be getting on and off. It is impossible…"

Kreesat placed his left hand on Sasha's shoulder and leaned down. He smiled as he turned his heavy pistol to the left and tapped the barrel against Sasha's chest, as if it was nothing more harmful than a soup ladle.

"Irkutsk is no longer a stop on this journey, my friend," Kreesat said. "No one is getting on this train, and no one is getting off."

CHAPTER EIGHT

Dan Morgan was driving like a maniac, which is to say that his vehicle habits on the outskirts of Irkutsk were not much different than those of a normal day back in Andover, Mass.

However, his standard selections of American muscle cars—in particular his Shelby Cobra—weren't available at the rental counters at Irkutsk International Airport, so he and Peter had had to settle for the weirdest contraption left on the lot.

It was an olive-drab Russian UAZ-452 "vagon," essentially an ugly eight-seater van with a bloated round shape, exposed wheels without fenders, and the laughable moniker *bukhanka,* which, in Russian, means "loaf of bread." But Morgan didn't care about automotive fashion.

The distance from the airport to the train station was fourteen kilometers; according to Lincoln Shepard, who was sitting in the middle bank of seats behind Morgan and Conley, the Trans-Siberian would be pulling into the station in exactly eight-point-five minutes, and no one could say how long it would stay before thundering off to the next leg of its journey.

"Take a left there," Peter Conley said from the forward passenger seat.

"Where?" Morgan asked.

"Here!" Conley stabbed a finger at the windshield, Morgan spun the fat white steering wheel, and the van lifted completely off its left tires as it careened into a slim lane between high rows of Petrovian apartments. There was a breathless second while the vehicle just sped forward on two wheels, then smashed back down on all fours.

"Jesus!" Linc gasped from his seat as his head banged the fuselage.

"Give me a little more notice, will ya?" Morgan snapped at Conley.

"Hey, I'm using a Russian nav app on a rented Bulgarian phone and the cell service sucks," Conley said. "I think I'm doing pretty good."

"Actually, you are," Morgan admitted.

"Gentlemen, you'll want to know this," Linc said from the back. He had his headset on, and a smaller version of his Alienware open on his lap. "I'm getting encrypted comms from Diana, and she must be upset because she's making typos. She hates typos."

"What's the upshot?" Morgan asked over his shoulder.

"Funny choice of words," Linc said.

"Stay straight here for two klicks," Conley said to Morgan as he pointed dead ahead.

"The upshot is," Linc continued, "that this Deputy National Security Advisor at 1900 Pennsylvania Ave has confirmed to our own Mr. Smith that Major Maxim Kreesat's claim of control over Laika II is no bluff."

"I could have told them that," Morgan snorted. "Kreesat's a slime ball, but he doesn't bluff."

"Wait, there's more," Linc said. "The President's been on the red phone with Vlad the Impaler. Seems Putin denied the whole MIRV platform thingy on Laika II, until Kreesat took it for a spin over Moscow about two hours after his drive-by over D.C. Then Russian Space Command tried to regain control over the bird, but Dmitri Kozlov's been able to shut them out … probably under duress."

"Gee, ya think?" Conley said, then glanced down at his navigation app and pointed diagonally to the right—past the UAZ's bulbous nose. "Get ready to take a hard right, up there by the Stalin monument."

"Okay, Linc, what's the punchline?" Morgan said. "I know you by now. There's always a punchline."

"Yeah, but it's no joke, Cobra," Linc said. "Diana had no choice. She had to tell the National Security Advisor, who, in turn, had to tell the Pentagon and POTUS, who, in *turn*, had to tell the Russian premier, that Laika II's being controlled by someone aboard the Trans-Siberian, en route from Vladivostok to Moscow."

"Holy crap," Conley growled.

"That's right." Linc stopped looking at his laptop and leaned forward between the two senior agents. "The Russians want to scramble a flight of MIG-29s and take out the train—like *now*. Diana's only been able to hold them off by having the National Security Advisor try to convince them to use commandos, rather than bomb a whole trainload of innocents. Meanwhile, Treasury's keeping it going by getting Kreesat's ransom together, while Moscow's doing the same."

"Bastard," Morgan spat. "What's his fee?"

"Five hundred million USD, a *piece*."

"A piece?" Conley turned and stared at Linc. "He must be using my ex-wife's lawyer."

"Time check," Morgan barked at Linc.

Shepard checked the blinking icon on his iPhone navigation app. "Three minutes till the train pulls in."

"And what's our ETA?" Morgan asked Conley.

"Five minutes. And turn right! Right here!"

Morgan spun the wheel the other way and Linc slid across the back seat like a dinner plate in a missile boat galley—banging the other side of his head.

"Ow! Damn it, Cobra!"

"We're going to make that train," Morgan grunted as he stomped on the gas pedal. "If nothing else, we're going to grab Alex, toss her off the back, and jump after her before the Russian air force turns the rest of the passengers to toast."

But they didn't make the train.

Morgan pulled into the station with a minute to spare. The enormous building occupied two full city blocks—a beautiful edifice of pale, canary-colored stone rimmed in mint green trim, with carved white arches, its entrance braced by towers sporting Russian Orthodox ceramic caps. The wide thoroughfare in front of the station was barricaded so that drivers could only drop off or pick up passengers, but Morgan wasn't looking for a valid parking space. He figured they'd dump the UAZ, call the rental company later to come and get it themselves, and let Zeta Division foot the bill. He screeched to a halt at the curb right in front of the main entrance, just as they all heard the locomotive whistling its warning to those inside on the platform.

"Hustle up!" Morgan snapped at Conley and Shepard as they slammed the van doors, sprinted across the station apron, burst into the main hallway, and kept right on going for the other side of the building and out onto the platform. But as soon as they punched the second set of doors open, a blast of compressed wind slammed all three of them back against the glass, making their hair stand on end.

The Trans-Siberian was rocketing right through the station, hell bent for leather, its whistle howling like a demon and sparks flying off its iron wheels. Its thunder pushed scores of waiting ticket-holders back on their heels, and as the Americans gaped, many of the wailing travelers were raising clenched fists, shouting and cursing at the insane engineer.

And then the Trans-Siberian was gone.

Morgan, Conley, and Shepard stared after the receding rectangle of the train's caboose. Shepard spoke first.

"Holy moly Mother of God, what now?"

But he found himself alone, clutching his laptop on the platform as Morgan and Conley took off back through the station. He charged after them.

"Hey! Wait!" he cried. "Where you guys going?"

"Back to the airport," Morgan called over his shoulder as he ran back to the van.

"What? You can't chase a train in a Lear jet!"

"Forget the jet," Conley said as they reached the UAZ and he and Morgan jumped in.

"We're gonna hotwire a helicopter," Morgan said. Linc just managed to leap into the back as Morgan burned rubber backwards.

"You can hotwire a helicopter?" Shepard gasped as his eyes bugged and he madly buckled his seatbelt.

"No idea," Conley said grimly. "Never tried it."

"Look it up on YouTube," Morgan ordered Shepard as he gunned the engine and raced back toward the airport. "You've got nine minutes."

"Oh Lord," Shepard whined as he flipped his laptop open, stabbed at the keys, and prayed.

* * * *

Twenty minutes outside Irkutsk, the Trans-Siberian went dark. The train had just entered a rolling plain of high yellow wheat and descended further into a valley of wild Siberian bristle brush—a stretch of sparsely populated vastness in which no government telecom engineers had bothered to erect any cell phone towers, because, as the Kremlin had decreed, "There is no one out there worth talking to."

Under normal circumstances, this "dark territory" deprivation of telecom service of any kind aboard the express would not have alarmed the passengers, as they'd been warned about it well in advance, and some had even chosen the route precisely for the experience. It was difficult to get through a meal nowadays or take a simple commuter flight without some inconsiderate bore yammering away on his cell phone, so it would have been a quaint sort of pleasure to be forced to read or even converse. Besides, the train's engineer surely had some way of making contact with the outside world in the event of an emergency.

So, dark territory would have been a welcome interlude—except that the train was supposed to stop at Irkutsk, but had rocketed right through the station, and now there were scores of passengers stomping up and down the corridors, trying to find out why.

The train's engineer did indeed have an alternate means of making contact with transportation headquarters in St. Petersburg. It was an emergency, high-powered radio transmitter, bolted into his console in the train's forward cockpit, and similar to the emergency transponders aboard all modern airliners. Mayday situation? Hijack event? All communications failed and the oxygen masks flinging down? You could just flip the toggle guard up and slam your palm on that big red button that looked like Hillary's failed reset with Moscow. It was the same here aboard the Trans-Siberian, and with its engineer, Ivan Petrovich.

Except that Ivan didn't dare reach for that button, because next to him, perched on the backup engineer's fold-down stool, was a very muscular blond Serbian woman who was literally breathing down his neck. Amina sat there with her left hand caressing the back of Ivan's tingling skull, her short fingernails scratching his scalp. In her right hand she held a Makarov 9mm pistol, and she was running the barrel across her bottom lip as her cold, green, feline eyes scanned his control console, searching for his Mayday device.

"Now, where, oh where could it be?" she sing-songed in Ivan's ear as he tried to focus on the track lines ahead and not think about who the hell she might be or what she was doing in his cockpit with her muscular breasts pressed against his back and her hot breath in his ear. "Is it this one, perhaps?" She pulled the Makarov barrel away from her lips and jutted the foreblade sight at Ivan's emergency communications module. He flinched involuntarily, and she smiled. "Oh, it *is*, isn't it?" She sounded so pleased with herself.

And Ivan nearly soiled himself as she fired two bullets into the radio set, at such close range that burning powder singed his hairy arms and he was momentarily blinded by the flashes.

"There," she said with utter satisfaction. "Now we're *really* in dark territory."

* * * *

Back in the cargo car, directly behind the locomotive where Amina was terrorizing Ivan, Kreesat was once more ensconced in Cargo Berth Four, from where he was managing his extortion scheme. Dmitri Kozlov remained his prisoner, and had now been joined in that role by Sasha, who had managed to deliver a hundred and forty-six "female" passports as well as the matching passenger manifest.

Vlado Hislak, due to the ministrations of Amina and some additional nourishment, had begun to recover from his injuries and shame, and was now upright and stable on his feet, despite some considerable swelling in his groin. Bojan was out in the corridor, leaning back against the fuselage, and checking the springs on three full magazines of 9mm ammunition for his CZ.

On instructions from Kreesat, Karl had summoned the last two Serbians up forward—a pair of blond, spiked-haircut cousins named Spiro and Mako—and the trio were now blocking the entrance between the cargo car and the First Class dining car. They were fully armed and unabashedly displaying their weapons to a packed-in gathering of alarmed passengers.

As Kozlov sat hunched and deflated in the chair in front of the single sideband transmitter, awaiting the next set of horrible instructions, Kreesat perched on the corner of the metal table and ran a fingernail down Sasha's passenger printout. On the other side of the table, Sasha stood murmuring complaints as he tried to alphabetically order the passports and respond to Kreesat's inquiries by plucking the appropriate one from the pile to show Kreesat the owner's photo.

"Novello, Sabrina," Kreesat said as he looked at his list, which also noted nationality and age. "She's Italian and twenty-eight. Let's see her."

Sasha found the matching EU passport and held it up with the front flap open for Kreesat to see. The Serbian made a face. "Ugh. Not nearly as attractive as her name."

He continued on, searching for females of appropriate age ranges who could possibly be of great physical strength or at least considerable martial arts skills. At last, he got to the M's.

"Let me see this one, Montefiore, Elizabeth." Then he held up a hand to belay that order. "No, wait. This one, instead. Morgan, Alexandra. American girl."

Sasha, palms sweating and his old heart hammering—he knew too well that he didn't have Alex's passport in the pile and had no idea where she was hiding—flipped through his stack of American passports once, then again, until he finally looked at Kreesat's expectant expression.

"For some reason, Mr. Kreesat, I do not seem to be able to find this one."

"That pile is all the American ones? You are absolutely sure?"

"Yes, although this young woman … Perhaps I missed her somehow, or perhaps she was in the toilet."

Kreesat got up from his perch and started to pace as he tapped two fingers to his lips. "Do you recall what she looked like, this Morgan girl?"

"I, well, I cannot really say that I …"

"Of *course* you recall, Sasha. You've been doing this your entire life. What did she look like? And don't disguise her or lie."

Sasha, though he had some affection for Alex, wasn't going to lie for her and then most certainly die. He had seen what this Serbian hellhound had done to the policeman, Boris.

"Well, perhaps tallish for a young American female, and oh, rather short dark hair perhaps …"

Kreesat spun on Vlado Hislak. "Is that her, Vlado? Does that sound like her?"

"Yes, Major."

Kreesat clapped his hands together, looked up at the ceiling and laughed.

"It could not be!" he chimed. "Could I be so incredibly lucky? Could this girl be that bastard Dan Morgan's daughter, here aboard this train with me?" He spun on Dmitri Kozlov as he slammed his flat palms on the metal table, making a pile of passports jump and skid off onto the floor. "Doctor! You are going to shortly prepare a speech, which you will be giving via the train's intercom from the locomotive."

"What kind of speech?" Kozlov protested weakly. "What is it that you could possibly want me to say to all of these poor victims of yours?"

"They are not victims yet, Doctor. For the moment, they are simply guests. However, I must inform you that amongst them is a passenger of particular interest to you."

Kreesat lowered himself so that his ice-blue eyes could meet Kozlov's, and already the old man was again touching his chest in anticipation of another dark twist to his ongoing nightmare.

"As I told you, your daughter is under my control," Kreesat said. "Well, let's say that she *was* under my control, and she shall be again, but you are going to assist me with that."

"I … I do not understand."

"Svetlana is aboard this train. Yes, this is where I have been holding her all the while."

"I must see her!" Kozlov screeched, but Kreesat squeezed his forearm so hard that the old scientist winced and went limp.

"You *will* see her, Doctor. All you will have to do, is to announce yourself over the train's intercom and implore her to give herself up, because she is cooperating with a Western spy aboard—the daughter of an imperialist criminal named Daniel Morgan."

"And she will not be harmed?"

"Of course not." Kreesat actually managed to look offended. "You have my word."

The scientist sighed. "Then I will do whatever I must to have Svetlana with me again in safety."

"I know you will." Kreesat patted the old man's hand and got up, barely able to contain himself from rubbing his hands together. He reached over the comm tower, plucked the satellite phone from its charger and said to Vlado, "Watch them both carefully." Then he went out into the cargo car corridor, powered up the phone and called a number in the United States from the contact list in his cell. A young woman answered.

"Zeta Division. Please use your identifier and state your contact," said Karen O'Neal.

"Yes, young lady. My identifier is Major Maxim Kreesat, and my contact is Ms. Diana Bloch, if, in fact, she is still employed."

"Hold, please," Karen said, and after a few seconds Diana came on the line, her voice dark and snarling as if she were speaking with a man who enjoyed burning kittens. "Kreesat, this is Bloch here. State your case."

"You know my case, Ms. Bloch, as the White House and the Pentagon have informed you fully by now. But what you do not know, is that I have discovered that Mr. Daniel Morgan's daughter, Alexandra, is also aboard this train. You may confirm or deny as you wish."

"That's absolute nonsense."

"Well done. Exactly the professional response I expected. And now you may go ahead and inform Agent Cobra, that I have not forgotten that he owes me a debt of flesh. Tell him as well, that I am very much looking forward to meeting his daughter."

He ended the transmission with a flourish of stabbing one finger at the power module, then marched off for the end of the cargo car. He burst through the coupling door with a renewed spring in his step. Losing his primary hostage, Svetlana Kozlov, had worried him somewhat and pricked his warrior ego. However, the timing hadn't interfered with his plans, as Kozlov had no knowledge of Svetlana's true whereabouts or momentary liberation, and had therefore cooperated and the plot had progressed as planned.

Now, Svetlana was no longer a necessary pawn in the game. As a matter of fact, *no one* aboard really mattered anymore, for the sums were about to be paid in full. It was simply a technical banking matter, as well as the overcoming of some bruised national egos. Neither the Americans nor Russians would risk a nuclear strike for the sake of a billion dollars. They were spending such amounts on single aircraft carriers. Having one less boat would make no difference.

Kreesat appeared behind Karl and the two cousins, Spiro and Mako, who were standing at the head of the dining car and cradling Russian Krinkov short-barreled AK-74s. Past the trio, Kreesat could see that the car was packed with patrons, many of whom were still in pajamas, and none of whom appeared to have any appetites. Their silent eyes were glassy and troubled, a few of the women and children whimpering softly. Karl turned his head when he felt the major's presence behind him.

"Sir, should we confiscate their cell phones?" he asked.

"It isn't necessary, Karl. They won't be able to use them for the next nine hours, except for playing solitaire. We're in dark territory now."

"Yes, sir. And how are the negotiations going?" Karl asked.

"Exactly as I expected. Both the Americans and Russians are pretending to negotiate, while they argue about how to effectively stall the delivery of our funds and take us out. I've given them one hour for the transfers. If nothing happens, I will have Kozlov target the satellite on Washington first. But before I actually launch, I might be asking you to execute a few passengers, while the Americans listen over the satcom."

"Understood, sir. May I ask a question?"

"Of course."

"What's our procedure if the Americans and Russians decide to pay?"

"You mean *when* they decide to pay."

"Yes, when."

"Well, we'll confirm the monetary transfers, then launch the nuclear missiles anyway."

"We will?" Karl looked a bit confused. Even he hadn't anticipated such double-dealing from Kreesat, whom he'd seen stab more than a few men in the back.

"Of course, Karl," Kreesat said. "If we simply escape and take the money, they'll be hunting us day and night for the rest of our lives. However, if we take possession of the funds, and hit both their capitals anyway, they'll be so busy with the nuclear disasters that they won't even have the strength to pursue us for years. By that time we'll all have altered our faces and disappeared."

Karl grinned at his commander. "I would never have thought of it that way, sir."

"I know." Kreesat patted Karl's shoulder and called over Spiro and Mako with a cock of his chin. The blond cousins huddled closer. "Gentlemen, I want you to hunt down a female passenger who is aiding and abetting Kozlov's daughter—the one we were holding in the box. Her name is Alex Morgan, American nationality, in her early twenties, tallish for a female, with short brown hair and large brown eyes, rather attractive. I believe she's the one who embarrassed Vlado, so take good care."

"What should we do when we find her?" Karl asked.

"If she'll surrender, bring her to me," Kreesat said. "If not, bring me her corpse."

CHAPTER NINE

Mako was the first to die.

Having been raised in an eastern European machismo culture, he made the mistake of assuming that the Kozlov woman would remain as he had seen her before—timid, trembling and supplicant. He hadn't an inkling that Svetlana the liberated—unlike Svetlana the hostage—was a capable, resourceful and, now, furious young woman bent on revenge and freeing her beloved father. Plus, she was in the company of an American girl whom she'd just seen dispatch a giant.

And Mako didn't have a clue about Alex's capabilities either. He was picturing her as a typical spoiled American millennial—putty in his murderous hands, despite her having knocked Vlado Hislak out cold, which was surely by stroke of luck.

With his Krinkov submachinegun slung across his back, and twirling a vicious looking double-edged fighting knife in his fingers, Mako strolled from the First Class dining car through another car of sleeping berths. The passengers had been ordered to keep their doors ajar, and he smirked at them as they stared at him like impotent, trembling sheep.

Since he'd been instructed by the major to find the two women and bring the American one back, dead or alive, he inspected each sleeping berth, then moved on to the next—on occasion pausing to liberate some cringing woman's wedding ring at the point of his knife. This was a practice his uncle had taught him after the slaughters in Sarajevo—to the victors went the spoils.

By the time he got to the end of the second sleeping car, he was already bored. There were many more cars, and these women could be hiding anywhere. But one open berth caught his attention. Reclining on the divan in the sitting room was a sexy looking bimbo in a short, teal sequined dress and stiletto heels, with chestnut red curls and heaving cleavage. She smiled at him as he appeared in the open door, and cocked her chin upwards in invitation.

The seductress was Svetlana, the wig borrowed from a Polish Jewish Orthodox woman on board, and the dress and heels from a Slovenian stripper en route to a gig in Chelyabinsk. When she uncrossed her legs, Mako took the bait, grinned broadly, stopped twirling his knife and stepped inside for what he expected would be a brief interlude of fornication.

But as his leather boots hit the berth's small Persian carpet, he discovered that there was nothing under it. Alex had purloined some carpentry tools from the caboose's hardware box and removed a full square of the old car's floor boards, then lightly affixed the rug over the square hole with carpet tacks.

The carpet disappeared, and so did nearly all of Mako's body as he yelled and shot his arms out to both sides, his fingernails digging into the surrounding floorboards as he desperately tried to keep himself from falling all the way through. He screamed again when one ankle struck something below on the tracks and snapped in half, but he managed to hang on.

Alex emerged from the berth's sleeper and straddled the square hole—where little more than Mako's head was sticking up—and tromped on his hands as Svetlana got up off the divan and closed the door.

"I removed the toilet seat from the commode," Alex said. "I figured if we slid it under his chin, like a big porcelain collar, we could keep him here for awhile."

"Why bother?" Svetlana asked.

"Maybe he'll tell us something." Alex was looking down between her open legs at Mako's face, which was beet-red and beaded with sweat. He wasn't speaking.

"No, he won't." Svetlana frowned. "These types never do. I've known a number of Spetznaz and these are the same. And if we pull him back in, it will be like saving a scorpion."

"Not my favorite creature," Alex said. "He's got a rifle strap over his shoulder. Did he have a weapon on him?"

"Yes, I think it's down there behind his back. But please, Alex, do not try to get it."

"Oh, I won't. We don't need it for now, and there'll be more." She pulled her gaze from Mako's twisted face and looked at Svetlana. "Are we done here?"

"I think so."

Alex stepped back off of Mako's hands. His scream as he fell was snatched away by the wind roaring up through the hole and the thunder of the steel wheels below, which crushed his flailing body into bone meal and entrails, barely leaving blood on the tracks. Svetlana pulled the wig off and shook out her own blond hair.

"Well, that's one," she said. "Shall we go for another?"

"Yes," Alex said. "But first, help me put these floor boards back. I'd hate for someone to get hurt."

* * * *

Spiro's death followed shortly after his cousin's.

He and Mako had grown up together in Belgrade, where their parents lived in the same block of flats—a common cultural practice that made for brotherly bonds. They'd failed in the same schools, swum together where the Sava River met the Danube, dealt drugs together in Deponija, and when the Shadows were seconded to Russian troops in Chechnya, they'd raped young girls and castrated prisoners together. They were very close.

Having flushed out plenty of innocents and insurgents alike, Spiro and Mako had a routine. One would walk point, not really expecting to find every panicky prey, but leaving an odor of fear in his wake. And the other would follow along at a proper interval, so when the prey felt safe that one hunter had passed and fled in the opposite direction, the other cousin would appear. It worked so well. There were plenty of unmarked graves to prove it.

So, approximately twenty minutes after Mako had left on his patrol of the train, hunting for Alex and Svetlana, Spiro set off as well. A bit less casual than his cousin, he slung his Krinkov combat-style across his lower chest and marched through the cars like an old East German Stasi agent, jamming the barrel into every berth and bunk—scaring the hell out of the passengers.

That amused him endlessly. At one point he was about to call Mako on his cell and ask if he wanted to meet for a vodka in one of the dining cars, but then remembered they were in dark territory. Their drinking would have to wait 'til they both met up again at the back of the train.

He strolled through two sleeping cars, where no one was catching a single wink, and then passed through the Second Class dining car, stopping in the galley to snatch a roll, smear a pat of butter on it and carry on, munching away.

Then he entered the coupling between that dining car and the next set of berths, where, unbeknownst to him, his beloved cousin had already paid for their family sins with his life. The coupling was strangely dark. He stopped in the bumping, windy flex tunnel and looked up to see the light fixture was broken. Then he looked down again and …

A condom bloated with Red Savina Habanero chili powder, blended with eighty-proof Russian vodka, fresh lemon juice, and olive oil to make it all stick, exploded in his face.

Alex, having had about two hours' lead time before the Serbians had started hunting her and Svetlana, had prepared the devil's brew in one of the dining car galleys. While working up the homemade pepper-spray concoction, she'd sent Svetlana off on a mission to find a tennis racket, a condom, a roll of surgical tape, and a champagne glass.

From one dark corner of the coupling tunnel, Alex swung the tennis racket so fast and hard, she could have won the first round at Wimbledon. The condom, taped to the front of the racket, was also filled with shards of the smashed champagne glass along with the do-it-yourself mace, so when the chili-bomb burst in Spiro's face his skin was shredded as well, enhancing the horrific effect.

His reaction alarmed even Alex. He slammed his open hands to his face and howled like a pig being burned alive as the 350,000 Scoville heat unit chili seared his eyeballs and nasal passages, while the vodka splashed across the bloody glass rents in his forehead and cheeks.

He hurled himself backwards and bounced off the passageway door, and Alex hurled herself backward as well to get out of his way. Then, like some wild ball on a billiard table, he went careening around the coupling, frothing and screaming, his submachinegun swinging from the strap around his neck and banging off the walls.

Somehow Svetlana—who was clutching a ring of access door keys given to her by Alex—managed to crawl into the coupling in the midst of this melee, reach up, and unlock the boarding door. She gripped the handle and slammed it open as a rush of freezing nighttime air burst inside along with the howl of the train from outside.

Spiro, who was blind and in horrible agony, lurched toward the cool rushing wind, staggered straight out the door and was snapped away into the night at a hundred miles per hour.

Alex and Svetlana, both crouched on their knees and breathing like marathoners, stared after Spiro's dramatic departure, then at each other.

"Well," Alex said above the noisy wind, "that worked even better than I thought."

"Yes," Svetlana agreed. "But once again, we lost his gun."

"Oh damn! He had one on him, didn't he?"

"Yes." Svetlana reached out and pulled the door shut. "It was strapped across his chest."

Alex got up and helped Svetlana to her feet. "Well, next time we'll make sure to snatch the firepower."

Svetlana grinned at her. "*Da*," she said. "The third time is the charm."

* * * *

But Karl's demise wasn't quite so easy.

Unlike Mako and Spiro, Karl was a mature professional—a squad leader in the former Shadows who'd passed the stage of his youth where he could be distracted by lust or baubles. He was a killer, yes—he'd once set fire to a kindergarten in Grozny—but not a careless one, and when the two cousins failed to return from their mission to hunt down the American girl, he didn't go charging down train car corridors like some panicky boy scout leader.

He made some assessments, then went forward to inform Bojan that he was going to reconnoiter after Mako and Spiro, and that should he also fail to return, Major Kreesat should go to full battle stations. He was a dedicated warrior, and also comfortable, if things went badly, with the amount his aging mother would get from his high-risk life insurance policy.

As he began his patrol through the first two sleeping cars, he unholstered his .45 caliber PPZ, checked that a round was seated, and held it by his right thigh as he walked, trigger finger poised on the guard. The palm of his left hand rested on the hilt of a Dawson battle blade, tucked in a belt scabbard above his left hip, and the dark brown eyes below his fire red locks flicked from right to left like an oscillating radar dish. Unlike Mako and Spiro, he did not assume that this American girl would be easy to take, simply because of her gender. He had learned that the hard way, having sparred many times with Amina.

When he reached the Second Class dining car and found it empty, he began to walk faster—that is, until the girl he was hunting appeared at the other end of the car. She faced him fully—the description matched perfectly—and when she spun around and charged the other way, he almost charged after her. But then he realized that was exactly what she wanted—an ambush.

He raised his pistol, kept the barrel trained on her receding form, and strolled slowly, until he stopped at one of the dining car booths on the left and looked down, where Svetlana was crouched and clutching a large, black, cast iron frying pan from the galley. She cringed and looked terribly embarrassed, not to mention mortally frightened. He smiled and looked triumphant, as he turned the heavy pistol toward her and started squeezing the trigger.

Then a heavy hardware hammer came spinning through the air, cart-wheeling from the spot where the Morgan girl had run off into the coupling. It barely missed Karl's head as he ducked. It shattered a Tiffany lamp on a table behind him, and he jerked his pistol away from Svetlana and fired a shot at the hammer's source; the report so loud that it cracked a window in the car.

Svetlana instantly forgot her own safety when she realized Karl was shooting at Alex. She jumped up from the floor of the booth, gripped the frying pan two-handed and yelled something as she started swinging. But Karl jinked to the right and side-kicked her hard in the belly, sending her smacking into the booth window, where she slid to the floor.

By that time Alex was on him. She charged him straight on, reaching him in three long leaps. First priority: control the weapon. She deflected the PPZ barrel with her bladed left hand, gripped the slide, and spun left and backwards into his trunk as her right hand chopped down from above. It joined with her left and she snapped the handgun outboard, breaking his trigger finger inside the guard.

Karl yelled and punched her in the left side of her face, which made her see an entire galaxy of stars and lose her grip on the pistol, but his gun hand was useless and the weapon went clattering away somewhere.

With Alex still pressed back into his chest, Karl wrapped his left forearm around her throat and locked it there with his right, but she lifted her right foot as high as she could and stomped down onto his right instep. He yelled again as she shattered the delicate foot bones, and his throat lock loosened enough for her to squeeze her head down and out of his powerful forearms and spin to face him.

Alex tried to kick Karl in the groin. Karl blocked her kick with a left forearm strike and ham-handed her in the face with his pain-laced right. Alex hit him full force with an uppercut palm into the base of his nose. Karl took it like the beast that he was and managed to grab his Dawson and rip it from its scabbard, but Alex kicked it away before he had a grip on it, and the blade went spinning off to Karl's left and nearly impaled Svetlana, who was finally getting up from the floor.

Then Karl had had enough. He gripped Alex at the front top of her sweater with both fists, spun to the left and lifted her completely off the floor, flipping her through the air in a Jujitsu throw and slamming her onto her back on a dining table. The blow spewed the air from her lungs and she was stunned by the shock to her spine, but then she saw him above her and he was fumbling at the small of his back for something.

She spun like a top on the table, launched her legs up and smacked them together on both sides of his head, sending thunder through his eardrums. She locked her ankles behind his neck, squeezing her muscled thighs to crush him, but he turned his beet red face and bit her in the inner flesh. She howled and pulled down with all her weight and she saw that he had his backup blade in his left fist—he was going to skewer her right there like some sacrificial lamb.

In one remarkable motion, she jerked her torso up, reached for her right boot, drew her Benchmade ceramic knife and stabbed as hard as she could into his brain through his left eye.

Alex lay there on the table for a solid sixty seconds, just breathing. Svetlana had crawled out from the booth, and even though Karl was thoroughly dead on the floor, and gory, she was still clutching her frying pan. Alex spoke to her, though she was looking up at the ceiling and rubbing her inner thigh gently.

"I guess I didn't plan that too well," Alex said.

"Well, it worked out all right in the end," Svetlana said.

"He bit me."

"Yes, but I would have bitten you too, Alex. You are very dangerous."

"I mean he *really* bit me."

"I will find you some ice." Svetlana pulled herself to her feet. She was still wearing the stripper's dress, but she'd found a pair of sneakers somewhere.

"We'll have to drag him into the bathroom at the end of the car," Alex decided. "And we'll have to figure out how to lock it from the inside, maybe stuff some chewing gum in the key lock."

"But why?" Svetlana asked as she looked down at Karl, who was staring up at the ceiling with one lifeless eye, the other embedded with Alex's blade right up to the bloody hilt. "He is thoroughly dead."

"I know, but I don't want any of the kids on the train to see him. They'll need therapy for years."

"So will I," Svetlana said as she turned her gaze to Alex on the table.

"Well, maybe we'll go together," Alex offered.

"Yes," Svetlana said with a smile. "I think perhaps we both have father issues."

CHAPTER TEN

Kozlov's plea from the locomotive's intercom sent Alex sprinting to the back of the train.

She wasn't surprised that Kreesat would use him this way. After all, the old man was a hostage, being forced to employ his scientific talents to rain fire and brimstone on the world. Plus, he'd obviously just found out that his precious daughter was still alive, and that he might be able to save her. It was also obvious that he was reciting some sort of a script, but the tone of his voice emanating from the ceiling speakers was wrenching as he implored his daughter to break with this "female imperialist American spy," and come forward to survive and live in peace with her father once more.

But that wasn't what sent Alex hustling full tilt on a quest for some serious hardware. It was the screams and whimpers of women and children in the background of Kozlov's speech, and the old man's trembling warning that if she and Svetlana did not appear forthwith, Major Kreesat was going to start executing these passengers one by one. And just to smear some more foul icing on the cake, Kozlov also relayed that Kreesat had given Washington and Moscow one more hour to pay up, after which nuclear warheads would be in play. At least he was speaking in English so Svetlana didn't have to translate.

Still in the Second Class dining car—after she and Svetlana had stuffed Karl's corpse into the bathroom—Alex instinctively made to open a line to Linc via her ear comm when she remembered the damn thing wasn't working. She couldn't call Linc or Zeta, and they couldn't call her. Her cell phone was useless as well, as were any sorts of communications devices aboard the train, except for the satcom gear being used by Kreesat up forward. It didn't matter anyway. She didn't need verbal encouragement; she needed a squadron of Delta Force operators, or …

Oh no ...

That's when it hit her, right after Kozlov stopped talking and the intercom went silent again. She and Svetlana had stood there frozen in their tracks, listening intently, but now Alex spun on the Russian woman and gripped her shoulders hard.

"What is it, Alex?" Svetlana winced.

"The passengers."

"Yes, I know. He is going to hurt some of them, that demon."

"No, Svetlana. *All* the passengers. Don't you realize what must be happening now?"

"What?"

"He's threatening both Washington and Moscow with your father's satellite. But Moscow's closer, and they know he's on *this* train."

"How would they know that, Alex?"

"Because my bosses know it, and they've told the Russian Federation by now."

"*Yobtvoyumaht!*"

"Yes, whatever that means. The Russians are going to attack this train, probably with a squadron of fighter bombers. That's what I'd do. Anything to stop him."

"Oh my God." Svetlana's eyes brimmed up. "All these poor passengers."

"That's right." Alex gripped Svetlana's shoulders even harder. "But I'm guessing it's worse. Do you know how your father thinks?"

"What do you … ? I don't understand."

"How he *thinks*, as a scientist, as a planner."

"He is very clever, and he plays much chess."

"Then that satellite is going to have redundant systems."

"What does this mean?"

"It means that once it's been triggered to attack, it doesn't need someone on the ground controlling it. That person, in this case your father, can be dead and it'll still destroy its targets."

Svetlana hung her head in shame, as if she were somehow responsible for all of it. "Yes, this would make sense."

"Jesus," Alex gasped. "It's got a dead man's switch."

And that's when she took off for the rear of the train, with Svetlana tumbling after. She ran through Second Class sleeping berths, another dining car, then a line of Third Class cars where the Siberian and Chinese passengers were huddled upon hard slat benches—their canvas duffels and bulging luggage overflowing from the overhead racks.

Alex pushed on into the caboose, which was currently nothing but an unoccupied rolling workshop, with most of the tools unrecognizable except to a veteran train mechanic.

"What are we looking for, Alex?" Svetlana skidded to a stop behind her, gasping for breath from the chase.

"That!" Alex pointed up at a six-foot long railroad pike that was mounted on iron hooks, high up on a wall above a work table.

"What is it?"

"Fairly certain it's a de-coupler." Alex jumped up on the work bench and reached up for the pike, discovering that it weighed about sixty-five pounds. "Holy moly!"

In a minute, the two women were running back toward the front of the train—Svetlana behind Alex, holding onto the waistband of her jeans—the long iron pike bouncing on their bruised shoulders. They weaved back through the Second Class dining car, nearly slipping on a patch of Karl's blood before Alex reached down and snatched up the hardware hammer from the floor. They came through the door to the coupling and let the pike down as quietly as they could.

"What are we doing now, Alex?" Svetlana asked breathlessly.

"We're going to amputate the rest of the train from the front. No more hostages for that scum bucket Kreesat."

"This is very smart!" Svetlana grinned.

"There!" Alex pointed at a spot in the middle of the floor. Svetlana dropped to her knees and started slashing at the carpet with the Dawson knife she'd recovered from Karl. As soon as she'd gotten some strips of it loose, Alex dug her nails in and started ripping it back to expose the floorboards. Svetlana handed her the hammer and Alex jammed the claws down between two boards and started hauling back and splitting wood.

After a minute she could see the tracks rushing below like an escalator gone crazy, and right down there was the train coupling—connecting the dining car to the next forward sleeper, and, beyond that, the cargo car. It was huge and round, like two enjoined iron fists, and it looked much like the couplings she remembered from her dad's train set when she was still a child. She got down closer and peered at the locking pin and its heavy chain, then glanced over at the heavy pike where it lay on the floor.

Yes! Just crank that pin out with the steel teeth at the bottom, then spear the coupling right there and haul back on it. Too easy!

Svetlana started pushing the heavy pike over toward Alex, because she couldn't lift it alone. But then she dropped her end and jumped up.

"Oh no, we forgot something!" she said. "I return!" Before Alex could stop her, the young woman ran back through the coupling door and into the dining car.

Alex hauled the pike towards her, until the blade end was hovering over the hole. She got behind it and gripped the head of it, a bulbous iron palm grip, but she knew she had to be very careful not to lose control of it. If it dropped down below … game over.

"This game is over, American mystery girl," said Bojan. "Put that tool down."

She looked up. A man was standing there, one she'd never seen before. He was tall and rock-face handsome, with thick blond hair and a ponytail. He was holding a large automatic in his right hand, but it was down alongside the seam of his black pants. His arrogant Hollywood grin told her he didn't regard her as much of a threat.

"My instructions are to bring you to my commander, alive or dead." He raised the pistol and aimed it at Alex's chest. "I do not care which, so put that tool down *now*."

Alex hesitated. She already had the pike up at a forty-five degree angle. If she could just spear it straight down maybe it would somehow crack the coupling open and the locking pin would snap. She could save all those people on the rest of the train, even if she didn't make it herself.

"I am out of patience." Bojan's smirk went out like a light and he took aim at Alex's heart.

A blinding flash exploded in the chamber. Alex winced and ducked as Bojan flew backwards, slammed into the coupling door and slid down—leaving a smeared trail of blood on the glass. His pistol bounced on the carpet next to his twitching leg as Alex spun around to see Svetlana, who had also slammed into the fuselage beside the other access door and slid down on her rump. She was rubbing the back of her head, and Karl's massive .45 caliber pistol was lying near one of her feet. She had killed Bojan with it, but it had also knocked her flat on her ass.

"That is what I forgot," she said to Alex. "It is a very big and powerful gun."

"Yes it is," Alex said. "And you made the first shot count."

Svetlana was about to respond, when she stared over Alex's shoulder. Her eyes went wide and the blood drained from her face. Alex snapped her head around, already knowing who she was about to see.

"I am going to cause you great suffering for this," Maxim Kreesat said in a curdling growl. He was standing above Bojan's body while holding a large handgun on them, and his expression was murderous. "I worked with this man for a decade. He was like a brother to me. And I am also assuming that you are the reasons I have not heard from the rest of my men."

Alex and Svetlana remained frozen like ice sculptures, saying nothing.

"Get on your knees and put your hands behind your heads," Kreesat ordered. "And while you are doing that, you can think about the futures you shall never have."

* * * *

Peter Conley was flying "nap-of-the-earth" at a hundred and forty knots and thirty feet above the deck.

This wasn't unusual, except that he was flying a Russian Ansat light utility multirole helicopter, a machine he'd never seen before. There had been a number of helos parked on the apron back at the Irkutsk airport, including a nice looking Bell 212, but only the Ansat had the keys in the ignition. Conley had stuck his head in the cockpit, frowned at the instruments all marked up in Cyrillic, but then spotted the shiny key in the slot and said, "Beggars can't be choosers," and jumped in and cranked it up.

Now he was careening along at treetop level, with Morgan strapped into the copilot's seat and Linc in the back hanging on for dear life. They were all wearing headsets and boom mikes, and Linc had just started looking around madly for a barf bag.

"You sure you know what you're doing with this thing?" Morgan asked as he squinted through the gray haze of a rising dawn, trying to spot any sign of the train.

"Come on, Cobra. You know I can fly pretty much anything that'll leave the ground, right?"

Morgan glanced down at the instruments panel and pointed. "Yeah, but there's no English on here anywhere. How do you know what's what?"

"Aw, helos are like girls. They've all got pretty much the same parts—cyclic, collective, main rotor, tail rotor. You just dip the nose, keep the pitch steady and biting air, don't overwork the rotor pedals, and kick her sides if she balks."

"That's a horse analogy, not a woman analogy."

"Whatever, bro."

Morgan twisted around and looked at Linc, who'd gone all pale and sweaty.

"You getting anything on comms with Alex? Or anything coming off of the Trans-Siberian?"

"That train's as dark as a plumber's handkerchief," Linc said. "I got nothing except the occasional burst from somebody's satphone, and that's encrypted so I can't read in."

"Damn," Morgan said and he turned back around forward.

"There it is!" Conley jabbed a finger out past the cockpit glass, then right away grabbed his cyclic again.

Morgan leaned forward and stared. Sure enough, in the distance at about three klicks, he could see the small red rectangle of the backside of the train. A line of its cars slinked forward from that around a long curve, huddling close to a squat mountain. Black smoke curled back from the dark locomotive up front, which he thought had to be from a backup gasoline generator of some kind because all these trains were electric nowadays. Still, it made for a good target marker.

"Outstanding!" Morgan grunted into his mike. "Get on her ass."

Conley leaned forward and hunched, as if indeed he were riding a horse at the head of an old western posse, and the helicopter seemed to lean forward and down as well as its twin turbines screamed and the main rotor sliced up the freezing Russian dawn air. The back of the train's locomotive grew larger and larger.

"Now what?" Conley said as he focused on keeping the strange machine straight and level. They were very close to the ground, and what zipped underneath them was nothing but unforgiving timber and steel track. One small slip and they'd explode like an ostrich egg on a cheese grater.

Morgan reached for the door handle, but he didn't haul back on it yet.

"If you can get me on top of the locomotive," he said, "I'll bet that's where all the action is."

"Morgan, that's nuts!" Linc sputtered from the back. "If Conley flies us over the whole length of the train, the bad dudes are gonna spot us!"

Conley looked over at Morgan for a second and flicked his eyebrows up. "You know, Junior back there's got a point. If we sneak up on the rear end and drop you on the caboose, there's a chance they won't spot us and you'll get down clean."

"Okay," Morgan said. "And then what?"

"Well, you'll have to take a nice long walk in the fresh air, roof to roof."

Morgan turned around to stare accusingly at Linc. "Thanks, smartass."

Shepard said, "Well, it makes the most sense."

Without another word, Conley crept up on the back of the train, slowly, methodically, jinking the helicopter as needed and trying to keep it so low that no one aboard would realize he was there. The train's noise would cover the rotor sounds, but if he swung too far to either side someone up forward might spot them. And then he was right there, just ten feet back from the rumbling caboose. Morgan looked at him and slammed the door open. A rush of wind hurled into the cockpit, threatening to throw the bird off its flight path, but Conley held on.

"God, Morgan, be careful!" Linc yelled in his mike. But Morgan had already torn off his headset and had his feet down on the helo's skids and his body half out the door. He looked back at Conley as the wind whipped his face into a weird flapping grimace and he pointed down.

Conley dropped lower, the skids about five feet above the caboose's sloping roof. He held his breath and he held the helo steady as Morgan suddenly released his grip on the fuselage and disappeared. Conley pulled pitch and climbed straight up twenty feet, then he looked down at the train and grinned. Morgan was there in a crouch, shooting him the finger. He swung the bird hard to the left and darted off to get out of range.

"Did he make it?" Linc was begging in Conley's ear. "Did he?"

"It's Dan Morgan, Linc," said Conley. "Of course he made it."

Linc found the barf bag and threw up.

CHAPTER ELEVEN

The cargo car looked and smelled like a morgue.

Kreesat had made Alex tell him what had happened to his men, which wasn't difficult to do, since Alex was happy to share it, though she kept her tone as matter of fact as possible. The Serbian major then summoned Amina, and instructed her to gather up a few healthy male passengers, at gunpoint, and make them bring the four corpses up forward.

But Alex had to correct his math, noting with a suppressed smile that two of his men were no longer aboard the train—one having gone through the floorboards and another having stumbled out an open door.

This made Kreesat want to slit Alex's throat, slowly, and he told her so. However, he was going to wait until the train was out of dark territory, so he could commit the act live and in living color, via Skype, after first making certain that Dan Morgan would be watching.

In the meantime, he had Amina gather up some terrified male labor and bring Karl and Bojan's corpses into the cargo car and stack them up in the corridor. They stank.

Alex and Svetlana were also in the cargo car's corridor now, on their knees, with their fingers laced behind their heads, and Vlado Hislak standing right there, holding Karl's .45 on them, which he really didn't need. Whatever discomfort was still pounding through Vlado's throat, testicles and forehead had been flooded away by his fury at seeing the two women who'd dishonored his manhood and killed four of his comrades. Between himself, Amina, and Major Kreesat, who were now the only ones left of their team, it was arguable as to who wanted these women dead more.

Through the open door of the Cargo Berth Four, Alex could see Dmitri Kozlov hunched in the chair that addressed the metal table. Upon first seeing Svetlana, he had sobbed with relief and tried to embrace her, but Kreesat had shoved him roughly back into the seat. A monitor sitting atop the single side band radio showed satellite tracking lines and a single blinking beacon, which Alex assumed to be the Laika II being set up for a nuclear launch. To the right in the dark corner next to the humming gasoline generator, Sasha sat slumped against the wall in the shadows, looking very small and gray, his sad eyes averting Alex's gaze.

She glanced at his round toed boots, and beside them the coil of rough rope she'd rigged from the ceiling hook to Vlado's neck, and beside that the large padlock she'd used to dent his forehead. But all of that was useless now; she couldn't get to it, because she was kneeling in the crossfire of Vlado's pistol, and Kreesat's.

"You have turned a simple business arrangement into an unnecessary international incident, Ms. Morgan," Kreesat said as he glowered down at Alex. He was leaning against the open door jamb of the cargo berth, his right thumb stroking the teeth of his pistol hammer. The corner of his right eye twitched. "This is a typically ugly American trait."

Alex looked up at him and smiled. "We are difficult, aren't we?"

"Very. And I am going to assume that, before we entered dark territory, you somehow revealed the location of our uplink station to your superiors. Is that correct?" Alex just let her head slip to the side and raised an eyebrow. Kreesat slipped a long commando blade from a belt sheath and tossed it to Vlado, who caught it with surprising grace. He glared down at her again. "You should have stayed out of the family business."

"I've heard that before."

"I am assuming you are wearing a Zeta ear comm. Your father had one of those the last time we met. I smacked it out of his head with a blackjack."

"And he took a nice slice of your ear." Alex smirked.

Kreesat's eyes narrowed further. "You can take yours out yourself, or I can have Vlado pry it out with that knife. Your choice."

Alex unlaced only her left hand from the back of her head, and popped out her ear comm. Kreesat extended his hand and she dropped the small, flesh-colored, device in his palm. He dropped it on the floor, raised one boot high and stomped down on it, smashing it to bits. His act reminded Alex of a Jewish wedding she'd attended where the groom had done the same thing with a wine glass.

"Mazel tov," she said.

"Excuse me?"

"Never mind."

"So, now you have left me no choice, Ms. Morgan. This train is obviously a tactical target, for both Washington and Moscow, and in turn, those capitals are tactical targets for me. Thanks to your meddling, they have not yet complied and moved my money, which means that I have nothing to lose. If you had not interfered, it could have been all so simple."

"My bad," Alex said.

"Yes." Kreesat nodded. "Bad, and shortly, dead." He turned and looked at Kozlov. "You may launch now, Doctor. And be quick about it."

Kozlov raised his weary head and stared at Kreesat with burning eyes. Something had changed in his demeanor, perhaps since seeing his daughter alive, or witnessing the cruel horrors of this man who had promised to help him, but was now his satanic tormentor. Alex noted a look of defiance—this old scientist was once again a father, with his child present as a witness. He was not going to do anything shameful.

"I will not," Kozlov said to Kreesat.

Here we go, Alex thought.

Kreesat cocked his head. "You will not what, Doctor?"

"I will not launch the missiles." The old scientist puffed out his chest. "I will not be your tool of mass murder."

"I see." Kreesat looked at Vlado and cast his eyes over to Svetlana. The giant Serb took one long stride in front of Alex, gripped Svetlana by the hair at the top of her head and lifted her off of her knees as she screamed and reached up to grab his massive wrists. He grinned and ground the barrel of his .45 in her temple as Kozlov's face went bone white…

* * * *

In the locomotive, Amina kicked Dan Morgan in the groin, and he wasn't wearing a cup.

Morgan had just arrived, after snaking his way from car to car along the swaying, tilting rooftops, and having lost his balance once and nearly been ground to a bloody paste on the tracks. But he'd made it, climbed down to the coupling just behind the engine, cut through the accordion flex rubber with his knife, and surged forward into the locomotive. He expected to find some sort of opposition holding the engineer hostage, but he hadn't anticipated this blonde banshee, who seemed to be Spartan's doppelganger, with a twist.

She turned to him, looked him over, realized that he had no firearm and tucked her own Makarov into a belt holster. Then she grinned and bore into him with a pair of arctic green eyes, came up with something long and gleaming, and charged.

They both had fighting knives—real ones. Morgan, having just experienced this with Spartan while sparring, still had a good sense memory of testicle shock, so the foot flashing up towards his crotch was met by his left forearm as he bent hard forward. The impact of her shin against his ulna hurt like hell, but it hurt her leg as well, so her kick missed the mark and punched his inner thigh high and inside.

The thought flashed through his mind that he didn't want to kill her; he wanted to take her alive. Therefore, gripping his commando blade point-down in his right fist, he punched her in the left jaw, which she shook off as if a toddler had slapped her.

Amina held no such sentiments about taking prisoners. She grinned and flipped her Gerber blade straight out in an epee grip, then lunged to stab Morgan in the throat, which he just barely parried with a bladed left hand. Then he kicked her full on in the groin with his shin, which lifted her off her feet, but elicited no more than a grunt.

She snarled at him in a heavy accent, "No balls."

He wasn't sure if she was reminding him that his target was female and therefore the blow would be much less effective, or if she was commenting on his character.

She slashed her blade across the left side of his face, and although he cranked his upper body backwards, she caught flesh and his blood flowed down over his collar. He spun his knife, snapped forward again and speared her straight on, right under her ribcage on her left side. The tip of his blade met something hard like bone, and she choked on a scream, twirled her blade into an overhand grip and tried to stab down into his carotid artery.

He blocked that with his left hand and somehow managed to get a grip on her wrist, pulling her in close, but she head-butted him so hard in his nose he saw fireworks. Still, he held onto her knife hand and cranked her wrist so hard that something inside it snapped and she was forced to drop her blade. And then she really kicked him in the groin, full on, and as he dropped to his knees she spat out a train of Serbian epithets.

And then she was gone, and Morgan was left there holding his aching package with both hands. The train's engineer stared at him with huge eyes from his pilot's position, amazed that the American, heroic though he undeniably was, had let the Serbian woman kick him in the balls ... twice.

* * * *

Kreesat didn't need to tell Kozlov what was going to happen to his daughter if he refused to launch the missiles—it was obvious. Vlado the giant was grinning and twisting her blonde hair in his massive left fist, and her body was suspended halfway off the floor where she'd been on her knees next to Alex. The barrel of his .45 pistol was embedded in her right temple, grinding her flesh, and Kozlov could take no more.

A burst of fatherly rage and adrenaline propelled him from his chair as he yelled something in Russian. His small, age-spotted hands crashed down on top of Vlado's gun hand— enough to wrench it away from Svetlana's head.

Vlado jerked back, surprised and impressed, as the old man snarled like a mongoose and pulled the gun towards his own belly with all his might. And Vlado, not being very bright, or considering the fact that Kreesat still needed the old man's capabilities, shot him point blank. The explosion, and the bullet's heavy momentum, slammed Kozlov backwards into his chair, where his legs splayed and twitched as he clutched the gaping wound.

Alex was already on her feet, as was Sasha. Just two minutes before, she'd caught his gaze, drawing his eyes down to the rope and padlock tucked into the dark corner near his rump. He, in turn, had understood, and had carefully pulled the rope toward the lock, deftly knotted an overhand loop, threaded the lock's thick metal "U" through the loop, and quietly snapped it shut. Now, as he jumped up from the floor, he hurled the rope and lock to Alex.

Vlado caught the metal glint at the corner of his right eye, and for one instant, it was a David and Goliath tableau. Alex spun the rope and three-pound lock in a vertical circle that churned to a blur like an airplane propeller. Vlado, towering massively above her, turned his lumbering frame and swung his still smoking pistol to bear.

Alex whipped the lock so fast it actually made a hiss in the air—then impacted with Vlado's left temple, where it punctured the flesh, shattered the skull, and kept on going deeply into his brain. His heavy pistol spun through the air and smashed into Sasha's chest as his eyes rolled back in his head while his arms and legs turned to rubber. He collapsed forward onto the cargo car floor like a grizzly bear felled by lightning.

But Alex had no options left. She couldn't get to Kreesat—the range was too far and he was standing at the other side of Vlado's twitching corpse. He spun on her, his expression molten and raging. As he swung his CZ99 towards her, she dropped the rope and prepared to duck to one side or the other, but she was framed by both corridor walls. There was really nowhere to go.

Sasha's first shot shocked everyone. The .45 pistol was massive in his hands, but he was a Russian working class hero, and he knew how to deal with a tyrant. The bullet spun Kreesat fully around and he reeled past the cargo berth's door jamb and staggered back towards one corridor window. Sasha fired at him again, but missed him and hit the window instead, which shattered into a hundred shards and burst outside the train into the rushing wind.

Kreesat made to defend himself with his CZ, but Sasha fired three more times in rapid succession, and the heavy impacts to Kreesat's chest sent him careening backwards and out the shattered window. The last thing anyone saw of him were his boot soles, just for a flashing second.

Alex looked at the open maw of the window, its frame hemmed with ragged glass shards, and then at Sasha, who was lowering the pistol and breathing very hard. He looked back at her, his expression neither triumphant nor remorseful, and said, "Boris was my friend."

Svetlana, weeping softly, was kneeling next to her father and cradling his head. He was still alive, but fading quickly, his forehead beaded with cold sweat and his feeble voice full of liquid.

"You must stop the launch, Lana," he whispered.

"Yes, Father." She kissed his gray temple and held him. "What is the code?"

He managed to smile weakly. "It is your name, of course."

She nodded and turned to the keyboard below the single sideband radio. She typed in her name and after some seconds, the quickly flying beacon on the monitor image headed off in a different direction, and then stopped flashing altogether. She returned to Kozlov and held him again.

"Is there anything else, Father?"

"Yes," he whispered. "The microwave uplink. Kill it."

Svetlana looked up at Alex, who walked over to the gasoline generator, kicked the power toggle button to "off" with her heel and then ripped the electrical feed from the comm tower. The lights flickered and went out. The berth became eerily silent.

"And there is one more thing," Kozlov whispered to his daughter.

"Yes, Father?"

"I adore you," he said. Then he smiled and died.

Alex's cell phone buzzed in her back pocket. She took it out and, without waiting for a greeting, spoke to Linc.

"We're out of dark territory," she said. "Laika II has been terminated, along with all the bad guys. Tell the Russians to call off the fighters."

She ended the call and turned as the door to the forward coupling compartment opened and Morgan staggered through. His hair looked crazy, his left cheek was streaked with blood trails, and another trickle ran down from one nostril over his lips. He was gripping a blood-stained blade in his right hand.

"Hi, Dad," Alex said. "What happened to you? You look like hell."

"I ran into Kreesat's girlfriend," he panted. "I don't think she liked me." He looked around at the carnage. "Where is my old Serbian dance partner, anyway?"

Alex jutted her chin at the shattered window. "He got off a few miles back."

Morgan cocked his head, impressed. "So, anything I need to do here?"

"Nah." Alex smiled, stepped over Vlado's corpse and went over to give her father a hug. Then she stepped back and looked at him, licked her thumb and smeared some of the blood away from under his nose. "Remember that old song you and Mom used to sing when you'd come back from those boring PTA meetings you hated?"

"Yeah." Morgan grinned. "The Party's Over."

DEEP COVER

CHAPTER ONE

As soon as he stepped off the elevator, Dan Morgan knew that something was different in the hallway. His hand found the butt of his Walther PPK as his brain registered what it was: perfume.

He could smell a few distinctly different brands lingering in the air. That meant the women they had booked had arrived.

The models were necessary for their cover. American arms dealers operating in their particular corner of the business would have a parade of attractive women coming in and out of their suite.

Peter Conley had been making those arrangements with local modeling agencies. He had a knack for it, though the task was tougher in Turkey now than it had been in years past. It was a sign of the ways things were going in that country.

First they came for the swimsuit models, Morgan thought.

The smile died as it reached his lips when he heard the cries from inside the room. His Walther was in his hand and he was running down the hallway before the sound had fully registered.

As he got closer, he heard more cries and shouting. Though the sound was muffled by the door, he could definitely hear female voices. Something was going on in the suite.

Morgan's key card was in his free hand by the time he reached the door. There was no time for a stealthy entrance. As soon as the light on the lock turned green, he pushed the door open and threw himself inside.

What he saw stopped him cold. He'd run a dozen scenarios in his head as he'd raced to the room and he wasn't even close.

This is new, he thought.

Peter Conley was sitting at the small dining table that had been moved to the center of the living area of the suite. Four very attractive young women in cocktail dresses were sitting around him, laughing loudly.

There was a small pile of cash in the middle of the table and everyone there was holding playing cards.

All sound had ceased in the room and five pairs of eyes were now on him. Morgan holstered his gun and said, "Sorry, I heard some noise outside and thought there might be a problem in here."

"There is, these women are robbing me blind," Conley said.

The girls laughed as Morgan simply looked on, still baffled by what he was seeing. Peter Conley was in a room full of professional models and was playing cards…

"Sorry ladies, that is all of my money that you will get for today," Conley said. There were disappointed sighs from the women. "I'm afraid my partner and I have got to get to work. It will be time to go in a few minutes anyway; our clients will be arriving soon."

The women got up and headed to the other room to get themselves ready to leave.

As Morgan and Conley moved the table and chairs back against the wall, Morgan said, "Who are you and what have you done with my partner?"

"Run of bad luck. And one of those women is a graduate student in math. She was unstoppable. But give me another hour and I could have won it all back."

"Right," Morgan said.

Morgan hadn't been referring to the card game and Conley knew it. Something had been different about Conley since he'd met a former Chinese agent named Danhong Guo, or Dani—who was now part of Zeta. They'd had some sort of vacation romance and now there was something complicated going on between them.

And whatever was going on between them had stopped Conley from calling the three women he knew and occasionally saw in Istanbul. That was not only interesting, it was unprecedented.

If they'd had more time, Morgan would have ribbed his friend a bit more. But Conley was right, they did have a meeting.

They neatened the room, making sure that it wasn't *too* neat. After all, the penthouse "Sultan" suite, the beautiful women, and the expensive suits they were wearing were all designed to paint a picture—a picture that would attract the right kind of attention.

They had also spent money like rich idiots for the last two weeks in Istanbul. Their cover had been good enough to get them their first client meeting, which was now minutes away.

Right on time there was a call from the concierge, telling them that their guests had arrived. He added that the men appeared to be good businessmen. That was a code that meant they didn't appear dangerous.

That was as close to security as Morgan and Conley would get on this mission. No guards, no pat downs. The lax atmosphere would fit their cover as dilettante arms dealers.

The men arrived at the door and Morgan let them in. He recognized them from their photographs and ushered them into the suite.

The two Kurds wore Western suits. The senior partner was middle-aged and bald with a greying beard. He introduced himself as Barnas. He was with a thin, nervous young man named Hilmi.

"We spoke on the phone. I'm Dan and this is my partner Peter," Morgan said as they all exchanged handshakes.

"Can I offer you a drink?" Conley asked pleasantly.

Just then, the four women came bursting out of the other room. The two Kurds nearly jumped out of their skin and then looked in shock at the women.

"Excuse me," Conley said. "Ladies, thank you for coming. I regret that we have to do some business now."

Conley led them to the door and the women made a show of kissing him good-bye. Morgan saw two of them press slips of paper into Conley's hand.

That would be their private phone numbers, Morgan thought, shaking his head.

Whatever was going on with Dani, Conley had not lost his touch. Maintaining a cover was as much stagecraft as it was spycraft, and Peter Conley excelled at both.

He returned to the men and said, "Where were we? Can I get you a drink?"

The two men didn't respond, watching as the last of the women left the room.

"A drink?" Conley repeated.

"No thank you," Barnas said. "We would like to begin."

"Business first, that's fine," Conley said. "If you can come to the computer we'll show you—"

"With all due respect, we'd like to see the actual merchandise," Hilmi said.

"We can take you to our warehouse now. Will that be soon enough?" Morgan said.

"That would be ideal," Barnas said apologetically. "We have pressing concerns. We are from Diyarbakir, which is close to both Syria and Iraq. The new leadership in Ankara insists on intervening in Syria. We have no doubt this is a pretext for the new President to—"

"Let me stop you right there," Conley said. "We're sure your cause is just but please understand that this is just a business for us. And if you have cash, we can do business."

"So you would just as soon sell weapons to our enemies?" Barnas asked.

"The only thing you need to concern yourself with is that we are willing to sell you the weapons you need to defend yourselves, or fight for your cause, whatever it is," Morgan said.

Ten minutes later, the four men were in the hotel limousine. Morgan was not sorry to leave the hotel. It was expensive and depressing. When he had a choice, he always stayed in the Old City, much of which dated back to the Roman Empire.

Their hotel was in the aptly named New City section, and when you went outside it could have been any modern city in the world. Why anyone would come to this ancient place and stay there was beyond him.

They headed south for the town of Zeytinburnu, where they had rented a warehouse that was near the waterfront industrial section of the city. They were only a few blocks away from the hotel when Morgan saw that they were being followed. The tail car was a non-descript sedan. Though the vehicle was unmarked, Morgan recognized it as Turkish police issue.

Like most drivers in Istanbul, the hotel limo driver seemed to think the gas pedal had two options: off and to the floor. What made the driver good at his job was that he was even more aggressive than the drivers around him, who all seemed to view traffic rules as mere suggestions.

Remarkably, the police car managed to stay on their tail. After a few minutes Morgan turned to his partner.

"Do you see it?" Morgan asked.

"Yes, I admire their professionalism."

That was the problem with establishing yourselves as high-profile arms dealers. To attract customers you had to attract attention.

And not all of that attention was commercial.

Well, that was the job, Morgan thought. Behind them, he could now see that the driver and the passenger of the police car were wearing the distinctive blue uniforms and caps of the Turkish police.

"What is it?" Barnas asked.

"The good news is that we are making good time, the bad news is that we're being followed by the police," Morgan said evenly.

"*What?*" Hilmi said, nearly jumping out of his seat.

"Don't worry, I suspect they are primarily interested in us. And since we haven't done business yet, I don't think they will pay much attention to you, at least not right away. My partner and I will be getting off in a minute. Stay with the car. I will instruct the driver to take you back to the hotel. Then I recommend you leave Istanbul."

As instructed, the driver let them off at the next light.

They were six blocks from the warehouse and the two agents walked casually on the sidewalk. Morgan could smell the salt water from the strait of Bosporus that separated the two halves of the city—and the two continents of Europe and Asia. Up ahead he could see the Roman walls that had protected the Old City for a thousand years, before it fell to the Ottomans in the fifteenth century.

Morgan regretted that he wouldn't see the inside of the walls on this trip—not with the police car pacing them. They were getting braver and coming closer, and Morgan wondered if he and Conley would make it to their warehouse before being approached.

The agents passed an olive oil factory and were in front of the electronics warehouse next door to their building when they heard the unmarked car pull over behind them. Two doors slammed.

"*Pardon, bakar mısınız*?" Morgan heard behind them. Though, he knew almost no Turkish he knew that was the equivalent of *excuse me* in English.

Morgan and Conley ignored them and kept walking until they were in front of their own building.

Morgan would rather be inside. They were far too exposed on the street.

"Dur!" he heard one of the police shout behind them.

Before they could take another step, Morgan felt a hand grab his arm from behind.

Apparently they would have to do this outside, he thought as he turned around.

When they were facing the two stern police officers, he glanced over at Conley. His partner was smiling broadly.

"Is there a problem officers?" Conley asked, his tone friendly.

The policeman closest to him fired off a series of instructions in Turkish.

"I'm sorry, I didn't get that. Do you speak English?" Conley said, though Morgan had no doubt that his friend had understood every word.

"I'll handle this," Morgan said and then he said one of the few phrases he knew in Turkish. It was a phrase he had made a point of learning in a number of languages. "*Hoverkraftımın içi yılan balığı dolu,*" he said as pleasantly as he could. Or, in English, *my hovercraft is full of eels.*

He heard Conley chuckle as the phrase had the usual affect and the two policemen looked at him dumbfounded.

Before they could say anything in response, Morgan and Conley sprang into action. Morgan punched the policeman in front of him as hard as he could, square in the nose. Disoriented, the policeman raised his hands to his face. His vision would be compromised and blood was already flowing from his nose.

Morgan relieved the man of his handgun and then clocked him two more times until he fell to the ground, unconscious. At nearly the same moment, Conley's policeman collapsed next to his partner.

Morgan saw that though the street wasn't exactly crowded, they had attracted the attention of several people nearby.

"Let's get inside," Morgan said. As soon as he'd finished speaking, they heard the first siren.

And then the second.

By the time Morgan had the key card in the lock to their building's front door Morgan had lost count of the sirens.

Stepping inside, Morgan said, "I'm not impressed by your plan so far."

As Morgan slammed the door shut, he could see three marked police cars screech to a stop and heard even more pulling up.

"What do you mean?" Conley said. "It's working perfectly. They are taking us *very* seriously."

CHAPTER TWO

"We don't have long. Keep them busy, I'll sort our transportation," Morgan said.

"I'll be upstairs," Conley replied as he barreled up the staircase to the small office on the street-facing side of the building.

Morgan heard the report of Conley's Glock as he fired it at the police outside. It was followed by the sound of return fire. The gunfire was occasionally drowned out by the sound of more sirens approaching. By now, Morgan reckoned the *Özel Tim* would have arrived or would be on their way shortly. They were the Turkish equivalent of American SWAT teams.

Morgan didn't want to end up in a shootout with such a heavily trained unit. However, given the number of police that were out there and the number of bullets that were already pelting the front of their warehouse, it wouldn't take much training to take Morgan and Conley down.

They would not shoot their way out of this, Morgan saw. Nevertheless, he looked back longingly at the crates of weapons behind him.

The warehouse was a nineteenth-century, three-story structure nestled between similar light industrial spaces and the occasional storefront. Thick, oaken double doors dominated the front. When the place had been built, the doors would have been used to bring in heavy equipment or carriages. Now, Morgan was counting on them to keep the police at bay for a few minutes.

The agents had stocked the space with handguns, assault weapons, and even grenades and some shoulder-fired rockets. Scanning the racks of crates, Morgan wasn't so sure that they couldn't shoot their way out of this one.

But that wasn't the mission.

Instead, he headed toward the rear of the warehouse to the car parked there. It was a Renault sedan. As European cars went it wasn't badly built—though, of course, it was no longer exactly factory original.

He'd had a French security company do some upgrades: bullet-proof glass, run flat tires, and armor all around the passenger compartment. Morgan had also ordered some performance upgrades in power, braking, and handling.

Thus, despite the extra weight of the armor, Morgan had no doubt it was the best-performing Renault on the road. Of course, it wasn't up to the quality of work that would have been done by Shepard and his team at Zeta—and the car lacked Zeta's signature tactical upgrades. But this work had to be done in Europe by a reputable company to support their cover.

Now, of course, Morgan and Conley would be depending on the upgrades to keep them alive.

Morgan heard automatic weapons firing from outside. That was intended to make them nervous while the snipers got into position and the *Özel Tim* made their plans to storm the building.

They didn't have much time.

Morgan opened the passenger door for his partner and then got behind the wheel and started the car. The engine roared to life as he saw Conley barreling down the stairs. "Morgan!" his friend shouted.

There was smoke coming down the stairs after him. Conley jumped in the Renault and slammed the door shut. "Tear gas *and* smoke bombs," he said.

The thick double doors shuddered in front of them. The police outside were hitting them with something that was pretty large caliber. They wouldn't hold for long.

But that was fine because Morgan wasn't going to wait. He put the Renault into gear and floored the gas. The car shot forward, straight for the doors, which shuddered again under the abuse from outside.

He hit a button on the visor above his head and the doors flew open—no doubt shocking the men outside. Less than a second later, the Renault came flying out of the now open doors.

Morgan saw the problem—or rather, two problems—in the form of police cars in their path. He had no choice; he had to aim for the small space between the cars and hope for the best.

There was a jolt and a crunch of metal as fender met fender and their Renault shoved the police cars aside, making a space between them. Morgan was thankful that, like Europeans, the Turks favored small cars, even for their police vehicles.

He saw police dive for cover as he threw the car into a hard left turn. Fortunately, the street was pretty wide—especially by Istanbul standards—to accommodate the trolley tracks that ran down the center.

By bringing the Renault partly onto the sidewalk on the opposite side of the street, Morgan was able to come around behind the ring of at least eight vehicles that were facing the warehouse.

Then they were back on the street and rocketing away from the small army of police. That was good. Had they been trapped on the street, they would not have lasted long. Armor—even Zeta armor—could only do so much. And if your enemy had you cornered and a limitless supply of ammo it would just be a matter of time.

It took several seconds for the first bullets to hit the back of the car. That was good; it meant their hasty exit from the warehouse had taken the police by surprise. It was seconds more before Morgan heard the first siren. That was even better.

Any head start would help here.

The smart move was to head west, away from the center of the city. The farther out they were, the easier it would be to avoid getting pinned down in traffic.

Morgan blew through a light, barely missing getting hammered by a bus. Then he made a hard right and then a left.

"Anyone behind us?" Morgan asked.

"No," Conley replied.

However, Morgan could hear sirens. None were very close, but they were on the move.

"Did we lose them?" Morgan asked. It couldn't be that easy. Not with the sheer number of cops that had surrounded them in the warehouse.

"Maybe…" Conley said. "Wait, I think they have us again."

"How many cars can you see?" Morgan asked.

"None, but *one* helicopter," Conley said.

That changed things. Losing a fleet of police cars in an urban setting was tricky, but losing a helicopter was even harder. Much harder.

"It's a police copter and they have definitely made us," Conley said.

"Are they getting into shooting range?" Morgan asked. He knew their armor was weakest on the roof.

"No, they are maintaining a distance," Conley said.

That was something. It was a smart move for the police. Shooting from a moving helicopter in a city was dicey, even for a good marksman.

Morgan wondered when the Turkish police had gotten so smart.

They were showing restraint here. And they had found Morgan and Conley at least a week sooner than the agents had anticipated.

They were *definitely* getting smarter. And given the direction their President was taking the country, Morgan wasn't sure that was a good thing.

Morgan gave up on making wild turns to lose their pursuers. He found a major east-west artery and put on the speed. Morgan considered making for one of the few highways but rejected that as too dangerous. Highways were easy to blockade, and once you were stuck there, you had nowhere to go.

"Morgan…" Conley said.

"I see it," Morgan said, gesturing to the blockade of police cars looming up ahead. Slamming on the brakes, Morgan threw the car into a one-eighty that had them facing the other way in seconds. He put on the speed again and made a left as soon as he could.

They ended up on one of the city's many one-way streets, and Morgan was going the wrong way. He had to swerve onto the sidewalk to avoid three cars heading straight for them, and then he made a hard right.

This time, he saw the police cars before Conley could point them out.

Spinning them around again, he headed away from the second blockade.

Two blockades meant that the police were coordinating their activities with intel from the chopper. That was not just competent, it was actually impressive.

"We'll make for the bridge," Morgan said. His internal map told him that the Bosporus bridge—one of the three bridges that spanned the Bosporus strait—was less than three miles away.

"Is that a good idea?"

"I'm out of good ideas, but there's at least a chance that they won't be coordinating out there yet."

Of course, even if they got to the bridge—and made it across—Morgan had no idea what he'd do when they got to the Asian side of the city.

One problem at a time.

"Get me a route," Morgan said.

Morgan could find the bridge but anything more than moderate traffic could end this chase in minutes. And that was a real possibility in a city where it was often faster to walk than to drive.

But they'd been lucky so far with traffic, and that little bit of their luck held out.

As Conley directed him, Morgan put the car through its paces. He was impressed by the Renault's handling. The French shop had done a decent job. Of course, some of the credit went to his suspension guy in Boston. Jerry had hand-machined some parts and shipped them to Morgan in France. Now the custom torsion rig was performing even better than Morgan had expected.

As they drove, Morgan noticed that the sirens were getting closer.

Significantly closer.

Morgan could see the towers of the suspension bridge in the distance, just up ahead and on their right. If they were lucky, they might make it.

And then he saw the blockade just north of them.

He made a sharp right turn from the left lane and flew through an intersection as pedestrians scrambled out of their way.

They had to get a few more blocks north to get to the bridge, otherwise they would run out of road and run into the Bosporus sooner rather than later. Yet there were police cars on every road running north.

Damn.

"How is it heading south?" Morgan said.

"They're on every street," Conley said.

"The chopper?"

"Pacing us from behind," Conley replied.

Then Morgan saw the end of the line for them. Just ahead was a boardwalk that overlooked the water. On either side were trendy shops in nineteenth century buildings.

Three blocks.

Two.

"So you either take us into the water, or we turn around and face them," Conley said. "It's a half mile swim across."

"I'm thinking..." Morgan muttered as he crossed the final block.

At the last moment, he spun the car around, putting the Bosporus behind them.

He saw a fleet of police cars approaching. They stopped about fifty yards in front of them. There was silence and no movement from their pursuers.

The police car doors opened and uniformed men took firing positions behind them.

"They seem pretty angry," Morgan said.

Before Conley could respond, a hail of bullets struck the car. Both agents ducked behind the dash as the front end and windshield took hit after hit.

The barrage lasted maybe thirty seconds and then the guns went silent. Morgan turned his head up and saw that the windshield was cracked in fifty places but had held.

Then he heard a voice from up ahead, coming from a bullhorn. It shouted an order in Turkish.

Conley translated it as, “Throw out your weapons and step away from the vehicle.”

“Maybe *I* should talk to them,” Morgan said.

“I’ll take this one. It’s going to require some finesse, and more than your one Turkish phrase.”

The bulletproof glass on their side windows didn’t roll down so they had to crack the doors open to toss out their handguns.

Conley spoke in Turkish to the dozen or so police who were approaching the Renault.

Police grabbed them and pulled them out of the car. They were facing at least fifty armed men, all with guns pointed at them.

“Did I mention how much I hate your plan?” Morgan said to Conley.

“Are you kidding? We’re ahead of schedule. And now we have them right where we want them,” Conley said as the crowd of police drew closer.

CHAPTER THREE

"Switching to a feed from a news helicopter," Lincoln Shepard said.

The picture on the large situation room monitor shifted from the grainy traffic and security camera footage to high-definition video of a chase through the streets of Istanbul.

The high-resolution image was a mixed blessing. On the one hand, the assembled Zeta team could follow the operation closely. On the other hand, Alex had to watch her father and Peter Conley run out of road with the sea in front of them and a couple of dozen police cars behind them.

The Zeta agents' Renault executed a perfect one-eighty to face its pursuers.

Even now, Dad can't help showing off, Alex thought.

The room got very quiet as the police took position in front of her dad and Conley's car. Alex noted that even Diana Bloch was holding her breath. As director of Zeta Division, she was normally unflappable. Of course, her father and Peter had a way of getting to people—even trained and experienced agents.

Alex was trained and had a bit of experience herself, yet she realized that she was nervous. Actually, it was worse than that—she was scared.

And then the Turkish police opened fire on her father's Renault.

She winced as bullet after bullet hit the car. Somehow the fact that the video was silent made it worse. In her head, the guns were cannons.

The barrage lasted about half a minute and, remarkably, the car seemed to be intact.

Lincoln Shepard broke the silence, "I reviewed the specs on the armor. It should hold."

She saw the passenger door open. Words were exchanged and then both Conley and her father stepped out of the car with their hands up, each with a few dozen guns pointed at them.

She relaxed a bit when she saw her father and Peter were both in one piece. A moment later, they were handcuffed and loaded into a police car and the image cut out.

"That went flawlessly," Karen O'Neal said evenly. Both in their mid-twenties, O'Neal and Shepard ran Zeta's computer, technical, and engineering divisions. Recently, Alex had learned that their partnership ran even deeper than that.

"And they are nearly a full week ahead of schedule," Bloch said. "Now the real work begins. Morgan, Shepard, are your resources in place?"

"Yes," they said in unison.

"We'd like to get on site as early as possible," Alex continued.

"This operation will be ongoing. It will be weeks before you can do any good," Bloch said.

"We want to be there if anything unexpected comes up," Alex replied.

"This is Morgan and Conley…" Shepard added.

Bloch thought about that for a second. "Good point. Alex, since you're running back office on this, it's your show."

* * * *

"Did I mention how much I hate Turkish prisons?" Morgan asked.

"Once or twice," Conley replied with a sigh.

"And yet here we are," Morgan said as the prison bus passed the gate and approached the main building. The structure was surprisingly modern—nothing like the nineteenth century dungeon in his head.

"You're just thinking of that movie," Conley said.

"Well, it didn't paint a very good picture. Of course, I'm also thinking about the actual Turkish prisons we've visited."

"Oh, yeah," Conley said. "But that was over ten years ago. The system is much more civilized now."

"If it isn't, I'm blaming you. And remember, if I don't like it, I'm not staying," Morgan said.

When the bus stopped, there was a line of prison guards armed with assault rifles waiting for them.

"Of course, our hosts may have different ideas," Conley said.

Erdoğan Prison wasn't fancy but it was new, with high concrete walls and guard towers in the front, with even more towers around the perimeter.

In preparation for the mission, Morgan had memorized the layout of the prison. There were three cellblocks that connected to a central hub of administration offices and common areas. The cellblocks radiated out from the center like spokes of a wheel. And even though it was newly built, the high walls and guard towers did give it a medieval appearance.

The design was loosely based on current maximum-security prisons in the U.S. and Europe. Of course, that level of security was overkill given the profile of the average prisoner, most of whom were journalists, scientists, students, and various civil servants who were all guilty of "treasonous" or "terrorist" activities.

There were also a fair number of former Turkish military in the prison. They had been plotting a coup—if you believed President Shakir and his people. Of course, like the last one, this presidential administration had used accusations of treasonous conspiracies to get rid of troublemakers.

If Morgan and Conley did their job, the administration would have one less troublemaker to worry about.

That particular troublemaker was an important scientist at NASA, and an American citizen who'd had the bad luck of visiting his sick mother when the President was feeling especially paranoid. Turks with ties to America were considered extremely suspect. And this particular scientist had skills that the President wanted— badly. Of course, the United States wanted those skills as well. And, moreover, no one in his right mind wanted President Shakir and his minions to have access to nuclear technology.

The guards herded the new prisoners inside.

Morgan had steeled himself for the worst but the initial processing into the prison was almost civilized. Their group was undressed and showered in full view of the general population. It was a classic fishbowl technique designed to humiliate the new prisoners and make them more docile.

By the look of the two-dozen or so other men standing around in the holding room, it wasn't necessary. This group wasn't full of hardened or violent criminals. Morgan had seen enough of those to know the type.

These people were scared men who knew they might not see the outside of the prison for years, if ever. And the way things were going in their country, Morgan couldn't say they were wrong.

"What?" Conley said. "That wasn't so bad. Better than last time."

"That's a pretty low bar," Morgan replied.

"Just a little more of their intake and we can get to work," Conley said.

Morgan knew what was coming and he was dreading it. "You know I'm not sure the changes are an improvement," he mused.

"Didn't you spend six months in a Russian gulag?" Conley quipped.

"Wasn't great, but they didn't try to pretend it was anything other than what it was. Sure it was a pit, but it was an *honest* pit," Morgan replied.

"Have it your way. Me, I'm not much for the cold," Conley said with a grin on his face. Like everything else in this prison, the grin just made Morgan angry.

The loudspeaker shouted something in Turkish and the guards ushered them into a hallway and then to a large open room with two rows of long tables. There were two clerks behind a counter and Morgan realized that the room looked like the DMV—except for the six guards swinging nightsticks.

An officious man addressed the room in Turkish. It meant nothing to Morgan, but he saw Conley listening with interest.

When the bureaucrat in charge asked the group a question, Conley spoke up and said, "We are."

A minute later, an assistant came over with a packet of forms and other paperwork.

"I got us copies in English," Conley said.

Morgan grunted. Both men knew what it meant that their hosts had English language material at the ready: there were more and more Americans ending up in President Shakir's new prisons. In addition to a scientist from NASA named Dr. Erdem, that group included journalists as well as tourists and businesspeople.

Like everything else Morgan didn't like about this place, that was a problem for another day.

Morgan filled out the forms, including the bank information for Dan *Jackson,* the cover that Zeta had created for him. For this mission, Conley was Peter *Bourbon.* Any computer search conducted by the Turkish penal system—or even the intelligence service—would show they were flamboyant American businessmen with ties to the international arms business.

Morgan had memorized his bio and had no trouble filling out the forms as the bureaucrat in charge droned on in Turkish about the rules for the prison. Of course, Morgan had also memorized the rules while preparing for the mission. Besides, he had already decided that, in a number of key ways, he wouldn't be following them.

CHAPTER FOUR

Alex Morgan tapped her foot impatiently as Shepard checked in at the hotel front desk.

The Swissôtel Grand was the best hotel in Izmir, Turkey, which was on the Aegean Sea, a couple of hundred miles southeast of Istanbul. At just over 400 rooms, the hotel was big enough for Shepard and her to move around without attracting too much attention.

"Lance, is this going to take much longer?" Alex asked, as petulantly as she could manage.

The clerk talking to Shepard gave her a tight smile and said, in lightly accented English, "Just a moment, Ma'am."

Just a few years ago, Alex knew, customer service staff at major hotels were mostly women. But things had changed fast in the country, and now women usually worked behind the scenes.

Progress, she thought wryly.

Alex made a show of rolling her eyes at the clerk while Shepard ignored her.

Though they were running the local *back office* for this operation, they were technically undercover.

In her last undercover mission she had pretended to be a barely disguised version of herself. This was different. Shepard had checked them into the hotel as Alex and Lance Jackson, the spoiled kids of wealthy international businessman Daniel Jackson—now sitting in one of Izmir's two prisons.

This required more acting on her part. She was a socialite with an impressive, if vapid, presence on social media.

The only thing about herself that she had kept was her first name. That was one of the things her father had taught her. Keeping your first name undercover meant you were less likely to blow that cover by automatically responding to your actual name—or not responding properly to the cover's name.

Shepard had done the same, though she'd had to train herself to call him Lance, since everyone at Zeta called him Shepard, or Shep.

Shepard's part was easier. He was playing her vaguely nerdy half brother, which was closer to his actual personality. He'd even been able to keep his trademark jeans, hoodie, and t-shirt.

That was fine, since Shepard wasn't a field agent. Yet he'd insisted on coming along on this mission. He claimed he wanted the light undercover experience and that it would be safe because it really was only coordination, logistics, and support—along with some on-the-fly hacking of the prison or any other computer systems.

Alex would have believed him if she didn't know for a fact that it wasn't true.

Shepard never left his computer station or his workshops, yet he was here for her father. Shep simply didn't trust any of his staff to handle the back office on this one. And he wasn't going to do it remotely. That was the kind of loyalty Dan Morgan gave and inspired.

Alex had beat her dad more than once on the shooting range—at least with a rifle. In time, she knew she could match or surpass him with a pistol, but she wasn't sure she could ever match him in inspiring that kind of loyalty. And the oddest part was that quite a few of the people who were fiercely loyal to Dan Morgan and would put their lives on the line for him didn't even particularly like him.

Alex watched Shepard and the clerk confer for half a minute. "Lance, when you and your little friend are done with whatever it is you're doing, call me. Better yet, don't call me until my bags are in the suite."

She turned and headed out of the lobby, her absurd heels clacking against the marble floor.

"I'll be in the restaurant…one of them."

* * * *

After the paperwork, Morgan and Conley had been issued photo I.D. cards. These were tied to their commissary accounts, which allowed them to buy everything from food, to extra blankets, to small refrigerators.

The whole process was finished by eleven and they were marched from the central hub to their cellblock with about a dozen others.

Morgan had studied the design of the prison carefully. Each cellblock held one hundred and fifty prisoners, giving the prison a capacity of 450.

It wasn't a large prison by any standards, but it was the second and newest prison in Izmir—and one of the more than two hundred human warehouses the current president planned to build in the next few years.

But the residents were only there "temporarily." It was a remand jail, which locked up people while they waited for trial, or waited to be charged—sometimes for as long as a year.

They walked down the hallway that had two open floors of twenty-five cells, each on their right. The prisoners they were with didn't seem very dangerous, nor did the men occupying the cells.

"Do you see the kind of people they are locking up?" Morgan said.

"Yes," Conley said.

"This is what they get for telling the truth, or standing up to the bullies in charge," Morgan said.

"Not everyone here is innocent," Conley said.

"Show me one real criminal," Morgan said.

"There's us, for instance," Conley said.

"What?"

"Technically we were trying to sell illegal arms, then we shot at the police, there was that chase through…"

"Fair enough. Funny thing is I don't feel bad about any of it," Morgan said.

"Me either, and we'll feel even better when we grab our guy and get out of here," Conley said.

Morgan smiled at the thought and relaxed a bit. Conley had a knack for lightening the mood when he was getting himself worked up. He knew he wouldn't be able to solve all the problems he saw around him on this trip, but he could hurt the people in charge a bit.

And he intended to. More than a bit if he could manage it.

The guards stopped them in front of a cell at the end of the hallway, nearest to the secure doors to the outside. That was Shepard's doing. Morgan knew the young man had complete access to the prison's computer systems.

Though Shepard could have hacked the system easily, it hadn't been necessary for this mission. Ever since the last president had gone on the first prison-building spree, companies owned by Mr. Smith and the other international businessmen who made up the Aegis Initiative had made sure they undercut the competition for construction and I.T. contracts.

The Trojan horses built into the computer network were the simplest of the surprises Zeta had helped place in prisons across the country. It wasn't the first time Morgan had been impressed by Mr. Smith's long game.

In some ways, breaking out of this place was going to be too easy.

Inside the cell, a very thin, balding, and scared-looking man sat on a concrete stool in front of the concrete desk that jutted from the wall. He appraised Morgan, Conley, and the guard nervously.

The guard barked something to him in Turkish and the man backed up against the far wall.

The guard spoke into a walkie-talkie and the door slid open. Before the agents could step inside, the second guard grabbed Morgan by the arm. It took all of Morgan's mission focus and discipline not to deck the man.

The guard said something and stuck out his hand, which held two hearing aids. Morgan immediately recognized them as "his"—at least the ones he had been wearing when he and Conley had been arrested.

The man shouted at him and then pulled away the devices when Morgan reached for them.

"He says, they are generously returning them to you, but reminds you that they can be taken away just as easily if your behavior is not good," Conley said.

Morgan gritted his teeth and said, "Tell him that I understand."

Then the guard—who Morgan noted had a nearly shaved head, a dark five-o'clock shadow and a scar on one cheek—held out the hearing aids and Morgan took them. He made a show of putting them in his ears. They were the old-style behind the ear aids and Morgan didn't bother to turn them on, since he didn't actually need them for their intended purpose.

They would come in handy later, of course, but for now it was only important that the guards see him wearing them.

Inside their cell, Conley greeted their new cellmate in Turkish. The man tentatively returned the greeting.

"His name is Tunca Guler," Conley said.

"I'm Dan," Morgan said, pointing to himself.

Conley and Tunca exchanged a few words and then Conley said, "He apologizes for not speaking any English."

The prison was over capacity, with three in a cell. Shepard had manipulated the computer system to make sure that their inevitable third roommate spoke no English. It would simplify things when he and Conley made plans.

"Tell him not to worry, it's not like I speak any Turkish."

Conley and Tunca conferred and his partner said, "Tunca is a journalist."

"I'm guessing a good one if he's in here," Morgan said.

"I told him we were businessmen," Conley said.

"Ask him if there are any other Americans in the cell block," Morgan said, knowing for a fact that there was one.

"He says none right now."

"*What?*" Morgan exclaimed. This would all be for nothing if their objective wasn't in the prison.

"There was one, but he's being punished. He's now in a...*sponge cell.*"

Morgan knew what that meant from the mission brief. The sponge cells got their name from the yellow foam mattresses that lined their walls. They were in the sub-basement of the central hub that housed the offices, medical, and common areas.

"How long has he been in solitary?" Morgan asked.

"Two weeks."

That was bad. It was a long time for anyone.

"What's he being punished for?" Morgan asked.

After Conley relayed the question, Tunca simply shrugged.

"Ask him the fastest way to get sent to one of these sponge cells," Morgan said.

"No need to be hasty Dan," Conley said. "They can't keep him there forever. He'll be back on the cellblock before long. They want a scientist, not a babbling fool."

That was true.

On the other hand, it wouldn't hurt to have a plan to get to their man in a hurry, if for no other reason than to make sure the scientist didn't lose hope. Conley understood the man's work better than Morgan did, but he knew it was important.

Dr. Erdem was working on nuclear power systems for satellites, and deep space probes. They could also be used for habitats on the moon or, eventually, Mars. He had the kind of skills that would give President Shakir a giant leg up on nuclear power and nuclear weapons programs.

If they kept him in solitary much longer, he might just start to cooperate. And if they kept him there too long, he might not be a nuclear scientist when he got out.

In any case, he was an American citizen and an innocent man. That was enough for Morgan.

CHAPTER FIVE

Morgan woke up cold and thirsty. This was more like how he remembered his last visit to a prison in this country.

He sat up in the bed, which held the only two items that were issued to every prisoner: a thin blanket and a mattress. Conley was already stirring in the top bunk and Morgan's internal clock told him that it was about seven, a half-hour before the 7:30 wake-up call from the guards.

Tunca was up and sitting at the small desk. His bed—an extra cot added to the corner of a cell built for two people—was already neatly made.

Morgan headed for the small sink and turned on the tap.

"No," someone shouted behind him.

It was Tunca, who grabbed the cup out of his hands. "No," he repeated, pointing to the tap.

The journalist had a quick exchange with the now alert Conley, who reported, "Water isn't drinkable."

"I got that," Morgan said as Tunca held out a half empty bottle of water and Morgan took a sip.

"Prisoners have to buy bottled water from the commissary. Tunca works in the prison laundry to buy his," Conley said. Morgan imagined that his pay didn't go very far given that the bottle in his hand was the only one in the cell.

Tunca offered the bottle to Conley, who took a small sip.

The agents would have to pay Tunca back when they got into the commissary. Zeta would make sure that their commissary accounts were well funded—as befitting their covers.

A few minutes later, the guards did their formal wake-up call, which involved quite a bit of shouting and banging on the bars with nightsticks. The prisoners were mustered outside for a formal inmate count and led back to their cells.

A half hour after that, three bowls of some sort of slop were passed through the food slot on the floor. Morgan ate on his bed, Conley on the concrete stool by the desk, and Tunca on his own bed.

"Ask him what he did to get here?" Morgan said.

After a brief exchange, Conley said, "He says he did his job."

"That sounds about right," Morgan said.

The slop was terrible and there wasn't nearly enough of it. Portion sizes, he knew, were set by prison capacity. And the prison, like the cell they were in, was a third over capacity. So 450 inmates were sharing food meant for 300.

Prisoners could supplement their meals with food from the commissary but you needed money to do that, or family that could help.

Given how thin he was, Morgan guessed that Tunca had neither.

"Ask our roommate how long he's been in here," Morgan said.

After a quick exchange, Conley replied, "Four months, but he says that he doesn't expect to be charged for several more months." There was another brief exchange and then Conley added, "Apparently, there are not enough judges to handle the new cases."

"Well, that's because so many of the good ones are in here, or places like it," Morgan said.

That was true—the judiciary had been the target of more than one purge. Judges were frequently accused of disloyalty or supporting the "terrorist" movement that opposed President Shakir.

The guards mustered them into the corridor again, then brought them outside to an open courtyard that occupied the space between two of the cellblocks. Morgan and Conley kept close to Tunca. The man could be useful as they navigated the new environment. And Morgan had decided that he liked the quiet journalist, if for no other reason than the fact that the man had pissed off the current administration.

Normally, the first day in "the yard" would have Morgan on edge. There would be prison gangs fighting for control and punks anxious to test the newbies. But there was none of that here, just quiet men shuffling around outside.

"I thought there were sports or something in these prisons now," Morgan said.

After a brief consultation with Tunca, Conley said, "Not in the political prisons."

"And I thought we could get a football game going with the guards' team," Morgan replied.

Conley grinned. "You'll have to organize that."

A moment later a guard from their block showed up. No, not just a guard, but the one with the scar on his cheek. Morgan noted that Tunca took a step back when the man appeared.

The guard pointed to Morgan and Conley and shouted something.

Conley turned to his partner and said, "Apparently he'd like us to go with him."

* * * *

Alex finished her last call to Zeta's local assets. She was nearly a month early but they weren't at all surprised to hear from her. Clearly, they had been in intelligence work long enough to not be fazed by changes in schedules or plans.

The network was small but would all do their jobs. The reality was the Turkey had gotten much "hotter" than it had been even five years ago. Agents, contractors, and assets of every kind were much more careful now.

Some had judged the work too much of a risk and retired, gone permanently underground, or had gotten out of Dodge. Given President Shakir's actions, they weren't wrong to do so.

Shakir had infected Turkish intelligence with his paranoia, but they weren't fools and were actually remarkably professional. However, the great advantage Zeta had working in Turkey today was the fact that Turkish intelligence was now busy investigating large swaths of its own population. Thus, they were spread too thin to deal effectively with real threats—like Zeta, for instance.

When you added in the growing radical religious sentiment in the country, you had a recipe for years of pain for the entire population.

Alex was nostalgic for her days as a naïve high school student who had thought the world's problems would be solved if the U.S. simply "waged peace" around the world.

But Alex wasn't there to solve the world's problems, or even Turkey's problems. She was there for her father and Conley, and for the mission.

When her work on the phone was done, she realized that it was a good time for her to officially "wake up." It took a full twenty minutes to put on the makeup she needed for Alex Jackson's "wakeup" selfie.

Alex had trouble getting used to her newly blonde hair, but it fit her character. She lightly mussed the blonde locks and took a picture.

She captioned the photo: "Woke up a mess, LOL" and posted it. In this case, posting the photo meant uploading it to the Zeta servers where special software would subtlety change her face so that facial recognition software wouldn't tag Alex Jackson as Alex Morgan, or anyone else in the real world.

It was something that Shepard and his partner in crime O'Neal had worked up, and Alex was grateful.

It wasn't just important for missions like this. Zeta now had a whole subdivision dedicated to creating online and social media material to support its agents' covers.

Now, in the event the overworked Turkish intelligence agency was keeping an eye on her social media, they'd see a self-obsessed daughter of a wealthy arms dealer and nothing more. It would help keep the authorities from getting in her and Shepard's way. For that, if for no other reason, the cover identity would be worth something.

Alex was impatient to get on with their work for the day, but keeping her cover meant appearing to sleep in and then having a late breakfast.

Alex called the concierge and made a show of asking where the best restaurant for breakfast was in the area.

"Do you mean lunch, Ms. Jackson?" the concierge said in excellent English.

"Yes, lunch, food, whatever," she said sharply.

"Of course," the man said and rattled off the names of three local restaurants.

"Fine, would you have a cab waiting for us downstairs in twenty minutes," she said.

"I can connect you to the—"

"Would you just do it!" she barked into the phone.

"Yes, Ma'am," he said.

When she hung up, Shepard was staring at her silently.

"What? It's my cover," she said.

"Of course," he said, with a barely noticeable smile.

Keeping in character, she rolled her eyes. Then she switched back to agent mode, "Wheels up in twenty."

Alex went back to her room and put on an absurdly expensive Dolce & Gabbana silk dress and ridiculous high-heeled shoes.

When she came out, Shepard announced that her delivery had come. It was a large box with the very American name StoneRock, which was a badly overpriced shoe store. There were four pairs of Manolo Blahnik shoes in her size—and five shoeboxes. The fifth box contained her pistol and four extra clips. Even though they had flown in on a private jet, she hadn't wanted to bring the weapons through customs.

Shepard had already received a delivery from a local electronics store. It was a gaming console, accessories, and some of the special equipment they had been using today.

Zeta had been shipping weapons and equipment to the area for weeks. And local assets would be sending it to the hotel as needed. As always, the operation was carefully planned.

Though Alex's outfit cost most than she had earned in all of her summer jobs combined during high school, she didn't feel fully dressed until she dropped her weapon and an extra clip into her Prada bag.

They left the room, Shepard carrying his backpack, which held the tech they would need for the day. The cab was waiting for them downstairs as they began their first full day of the mission.

CHAPTER SIX

The guards led them through the corridor toward the central hub of the prison.

"Dan, what is it with you?"

"What do you mean?"

"You're on edge," Conley replied.

"We *are* in a Turkish prison," Morgan said.

"Which is Disneyland compared to the last one we saw," Conley said.

"Better doesn't mean good."

They reached the hub and the guards led them down to a new corridor. Since this part of the prison complex housed everything from the infirmary, to the library, to solitary confinement, they could have been facing anything.

"My money's on an interrogation," Morgan said casually.

"Your money's always on interrogation," Conley said.

"And how often am I wrong?"

They were ushered into a small, windowless room with a table in the center. At one side of the table there sat a very nervous-looking man of about thirty in a suit.

There were two empty chairs on the other side of the table. If this was their interrogator, Morgan wasn't worried.

Conley listened to the guards and then whispered, "That's our *lawyer*."

"Is it too late to request an interrogation?" Morgan replied.

As a rule, he wasn't a big fan of lawyers. But in this country he imagined that all of the good ones were in prisons like this one. Anyone who was left he assumed was either part of the president's corrupt system, or ineffectual and afraid of his or her own shadow.

Judging by the sweat on their lawyer's forehead, Morgan could guess what kind of man this one was.

He stood up and offered his hand. "I'm Nadim Akan. Your company has engaged my services." He handed them each a business card. Akan's name was on it, as well as the name of the best and most expensive law firm in Istanbul.

"We appreciate you coming out so soon," Conley said.

"Your CEO was adamant that I see you as soon as possible. I'm frankly surprised that the prison allowed it. In cases like yours, it is weeks or months before the first consultation."

"Well, our employer is very determined, and she has a way of cutting through red tape," Morgan said. Of course, that was a fair description of Diana Bloch. She was the director of Zeta Division and he knew she was the one who had leaned on the warden or whoever had allowed this meeting.

"We—" Conley began.

"We're glad you're here. We're innocent and we'd like to clear this thing up as soon as possible," Morgan interrupted.

"Certainly, when you are charged, we can plead your innocence…" Akan let the words trail off.

"Good, because we are *completely* innocent," Morgan declared.

The man was somewhere between stricken and confused. "Of course, you haven't been charged, but your arrest was on the news. There was video of the chase."

"Wasn't us," Morgan said, feeling Conley's eyes glaring at him.

"The video was very clear. And the prosecutor seems confident," Akan said.

"Mistaken identity," Morgan replied. "Or perhaps a frame-up. It could be a conspiracy."

"I see," Akan said.

"So while we wait for the charges perhaps you can pursue that angle."

"What do you mean?" Akan asked.

"You must have investigators. Please have them work on proving our innocence. No need to come back until you have something solid."

Morgan let that hang in the air and then said, "Otherwise, we're done here." Then he stood up. Akan followed suit, as did Conley.

As they shook hands Morgan said, "We have absolute faith in you."

On the way back to the cellblock, Conley said, "You didn't have to do that."

"I was perfectly nice," Morgan said.

"You terrified him. Then you asked him to investigate a wide ranging conspiracy to frame us."

"Given what's going on in this country, he'll be lucky if that's the worst thing that happens to him this year. Plus, it wouldn't hurt him to toughen up a bit."

"What is it with you on this mission?" Conley said.

"Like I said, we are in a Turkish prison," Morgan replied.

"That's not it and you know it," Conley said.

There was a moment of silence between them.

"What is it, Dan?"

Morgan sighed and said, "It's this place. Not the prison, which is better than I expected. But the country. Fifteen years ago we did something we thought was important to the U.S. and to NATO. It was also supposed to make sure that things got better here, or at least didn't get worse."

"Like all of our old missions. We did our best. We'll never know what we prevented," Conley said. "That's the job and you know it. There are no guarantees. We did the right thing then, that's all we get."

"You're right but I can't help feeling like we're cleaning up the same mess again," Morgan said.

"It wouldn't be the first time we did that. But you know this isn't quite the same mess. Shakir is a garden variety jackass tyrant, but he's also riding a religious wave that was barely a ripple fifteen years ago, at least here."

That was true. Like most of his ilk, Shakir had the heart of a petty dictator, but the slow and steady radicalization of the country had long roots. He and his predecessor had stoked that fire but they didn't start it.

"Yeah, yeah, but this place still pisses me off. And I'm telling you right now, if we're back here in another fifteen years, I get the top bunk."

* * * *

As they got into the cab, Alex called out, "The clock tower, please."

The driver didn't respond, nor did he pull the cab away from the hotel.

"Did you hear? The clock tower," Shepard added.

"Yes, the clock tower," the driver said in accented English.

This had been part of the briefing material. Drivers, among others, would usually not speak directly to a woman if she were with a man.

The more charitable travel guides claimed that it was out of "respect." It ensured that there could be no male behavior that could in any way be misinterpreted as flirting.

Maybe the driver *was* showing respect. But to Alex it seemed like he was showing it to Shepard, not her.

The tower was a beautiful turn-of-the-century stone structure that rose out of a large courtyard and was surrounded by fountains. As soon as she got there she took a number of selfies. And then she had her "brother" take more pictures of her.

Even she was annoyed by Alex Jackson's behavior—using a beautiful historical structure as a backdrop for inane pictures of herself.

They made their way west to a public park near a north-south section of a four-lane highway that was one of the biggest state roads in the country—running east to west through central Turkey. On the east side of the highway was the Izmir prison. In addition to hardened criminals it was also home to one of the largest female prison populations in the country. Consequently, it also housed quite a few children who were being raised by their imprisoned mothers.

On the west side of the highway was the park. At the north end of the park stood Erdoğan Prison, which currently contained her father, Conley, and one important nuclear scientist. Alex and Shepard got as close as they could while still staying in the park.

The open space, fields, and trees could have been any park in the West. However, Alex saw that a small but significant percentage of the women were wearing traditional headscarves.

That was important because as little as five years ago that percentage would have been zero, or very close to it. The eastern provinces of Turkey near the Syria, Iraq, and Iran borders had always been the most conservative areas in the historically secular Turkey. Thus, in the east, headscarves were not unusual. But the fact that the traditional headgear had made it this far west showed how far the country had come in its transformation. Alex thought that in five or more years, this city would look quite different.

Near the northern edge of the public park, they could see the walls of her father's prison. Shepard became more alert and started checking his phone.

Erdoğan Prison was named after the last president, and the prison grounds were built on what had been part of the public park less than two years ago.

Taking charge, Shepard guided Alex along the central path and put his backpack down against a streetlight post. He fumbled inside the pack and then pulled out a device about the size of a phone but a little thicker. She noticed that it was exactly the same shade of green as the light pole itself.

She saw Shepard place the device on the pole. It held itself in place and the matching color made it nearly disappear.

Alex knew it was some sort of a comm signal booster that would come in handy for the last phase of the mission.

"Is that high enough to do any good?" Alex asked.

"It doesn't matter where I put it, it makes the whole streetlight an antenna," Shepard said.

Alex was impressed but not surprised.

They repeated the operation five more times, the prison's concrete walls looming in the distance.

Just when Alex had judged that they'd spent enough time that close to the prison, Shepard announced they were finished. They headed south and out of the park, grabbing a cab for their last stop of the day.

At the waterfront, they had lunch at one of the upscale restaurants with a view of the Aegean Sea. The seaside was lined with hotels, restaurants, cafes and shops. Alex realized it was quite beautiful. Izmir had been a major international port since the seventeenth century, and was a nice mix of the old and new worlds.

After lunch, they headed for the harbor. Alex had studied the mission briefing materials, but she wanted to see the roads, access points, and ship traffic for herself.

They had barely begun when she turned to Shepard and said, "We're being followed."

To his credit, his voice was steady when he said, "How long?"

"I saw two men watching us as we went into the restaurant. They waited and followed us out," she said.

"Do you think we need help?" he asked.

"Not sure, but I am sure we don't want a big fuss. We can't afford the attention," she said.

"So what's the play?" he asked.

Shepard was completely in control when it came to technology and computer work, but he was far from a field agent. And while Alex was the youngest agent at Zeta, she was much more qualified to handle things if the situation got rough.

And how rough it got depended on their new friends' motives. She thought terrorism was unlikely. It was a growing problem near the Syrian and Iraqi borders, and also in Istanbul and Ankara. But terrorists still tended to leave the western coastal areas alone.

Even if she ruled out terrorism-based kidnapping or mayhem, that still left a few options and none of them were particularly good.

"Let's head for the pier," Alex said. Shepard nodded and they walked toward the ferry slips. "Could be terrorists, petty crooks, police, or intelligence."

"How do we find out?" Shepard said.

Alex saw the spot she wanted, a deserted alley between a ferry terminal and a large hotel.

"I say we ask them," she replied.

CHAPTER SEVEN

At the commissary, Morgan and Conley grabbed blankets, pillows and as much food as they could carry. The food was mostly bread, jam, and crackers of different sorts. And, of course, they bought at least a week's worth of bottled water.

The agents avoided the larger and more expensive items. They could certainly afford them given their generous commissary accounts, but Tunca had explained that the guards would simply take anything of value sooner or later.

The guards would give them no reason. It would be simple theft.

Morgan wouldn't have minded replacing the items as needed, but a cycle of expensive purchases and theft from the guards would bring the kind of attention they were trying to avoid.

The blankets would make them more comfortable, and they could subsist on the commissary food if they had to. Of course, there was always the prison food that came to their cell three times a day.

Back in the cell, Tunca was near tears when he saw what the agents had brought and offered to share with him.

The man's gratitude made Morgan uncomfortable. The few dollars in commissary items were nothing to Morgan and Conley. Yet Tunca had given his last few sips of drinkable water to men he did not know.

After lunch they were ushered into the prison yard. Morgan and Conley found a small concrete table, while their cellmate checked in with some of the other inmates.

When the journalist returned, he said through Conley, "The American scientist, he is still in one of the sponge cells."

Morgan didn't like that. Two weeks was too long for a man to be in solitary. Depending on the person, the effects could soon start to go from temporary to lasting.

And Dr. Erdem's ability to withstand the isolation would be diminished if he had no hope of release.

To Tunca, the agents merely nodded at the news and Conley pulled out his great find from the commissary: a deck of playing cards.

The men agreed on poker, which Conley explained was extremely popular in Turkey. Tunca introduced them to a few Turkish variations and they passed an hour. As they were wrapping up, Conley relayed that tomorrow Tunca would teach them a game called *Maça Kizi,* some sort of a Turkish version of Hearts.

That seemed to please Conley, who quickly grew bored with card games that were too simple. Even nominal betting would have made the game more interesting, but that was a bad idea. The guards tolerated the cards but Morgan knew that any form of gambling was strictly forbidden—for some sort of religious reason.

After the game, Morgan had Conley ask Tunca for his story.

The journalist sat quietly and then gave his reply, which Conley relayed. "He says he worked for the *Hurriyet,* it's the largest newspaper in the country. He was investigating leaked emails that showed a connection between Turkey's energy minister and a corrupt scheme to buy oil from various forbidden terrorist groups in the Middle East. Because of his articles he was arrested on charges of 'terrorism' and 'anti-state' activity."

Tunca and Conley chatted a bit more, and then Conley said, "He doesn't expect his case to go to trial. He thinks they will keep him here, and then he will simply disappear."

From the president's point of view that made sense if the report was true and especially if the president himself was involved or had authorized the deals. Given the iron grip he had on the country, Morgan assumed Shakir was pulling the strings.

"Tell him I'm sorry to hear that," Morgan said.

Tunca shrugged, as if to say *that is just the way it is here.*

Morgan recognized the shrug from countless places around the world. It was the shrug of people who didn't have much hope.

And given what he knew about the way this country was going, Morgan wasn't sure there was much hope of things getting better, at least in the short term.

The three men were silent on the way back to their cell. On the outside, Morgan was just another resigned prisoner heading back to his cell. On the inside, he felt a pit of anger starting in his stomach.

The snarling face of their guard, the one with the scar on his cheek, didn't help Morgan's mood. Just as the man opened the cell door, he put a hand on Tunca's shoulder while the two agents stepped inside.

Morgan turned around to see the bars slide shut, with Tunca on the other side.

"What's going on?" Morgan said to Conley.

Tunca said a few words and Conley said, "Interrogation."

In the second before he was pulled away, Tunca's eyes met Morgan's and the journalist gave a little shrug.

Morgan watched them go, that pit of anger in his stomach getting bigger by the second.

* * * *

"What should I do?" Shepard asked.

Alex kept her expression neutral and her voice calm. "When it starts, step away. I'll need some room. And yell if you see either one of them draw a gun," she said.

"Okay," Shepard said. The young man was remarkably cool. He was nervous, but not exactly scared—which was a good enough description of how she was feeling herself. That was good—being too scared or too confident during a fight could get you hurt or killed.

Alex and Shepard turned into the alley and Alex saw that it was a dead end. That meant there was only one way out—through the two men who were behind them.

That was fine with Alex; she just hoped that Shepard kept out of the way. For one, she didn't want to see him get hurt. Secondly, she needed him all in one piece to complete the mission.

"I see them now," Shepard said. By now it was impossible to miss them. They were no more than fifteen paces behind Alex and Shepard.

"Any chance we'll get caught on a security camera?" Alex asked quietly.

"No," Shepard replied. "Zeta will be tracking us by our phones and watching the feeds. They'll cut them if there's anything we wouldn't want the authorities to see."

That was good. It meant that Alex could do what she had to do without worrying about having the police see the footage or—worse—having it end up on the evening news.

The men's footsteps now echoed in the alley. They were walking briskly, and she estimated they were now less than ten paces behind. That's when she turned quickly on her heels to face them and said, "Can I help you?"

That stopped the two men cold. They were of average height, and by the dull, menacing expressions on their faces, they were of *maybe* average intelligence. They also didn't move like military men or trained fighters.

As instructed, Shepard moved sideways, ending up with his back against the alley wall as Alex kept herself in the center of the space. To her surprise, the men ignored her and kept their eyes on Shepard.

Because of course they did…

Like the cab drivers, they would only deal with the man she was with. *You've got to be kidding me,* she thought.

Shepard spoke up. "Maybe you can help us, we got turned around."

The men responded with something incomprehensible in Turkish. Shepard continued, "We're trying to find Tanis. There's this map room that's supposed to get us to the Well of Souls."

Alex smiled as the men each pulled out a small club—no, a blackjack. *So a robbery then,* she thought. *Or worse.*

She said a silent thanks to her Zeta martial arts instructor Alicia Schmitt, who had made her train in the kind of clothes she'd be wearing on this mission: dresses and high heels. The dresses actually made movement easier but the heels had been a bit of a challenge at first.

Alex launched herself at the man closest to her. She considered her options, running through several different scenarios for a first strike. In the end, she decided not to get too fancy. She had nothing to prove, and she didn't want to take any chances.

Alex brought her Prada bag around in a long arc, the weight of the pistol adding quite a bit to the force of the blow when the bag made solid contact with the side of the man's head.

The thud was loud and the man dropped to the pavement.

The second man turned in surprise and Alex saw that the dull look on his face definitely wasn't an act. Of course, that didn't mean he wasn't dangerous.

Once he realized what had happened, he re-directed and swung the blackjack at Alex.

She side-stepped the blow and saw that the purse and gun wouldn't be much help here. She tossed the purse toward Shepard and assumed a ready position.

He lunged forward and swung the blackjack again. She dodged by pulling her head back and to one side. He missed but his weapon came within an inch of her face.

That was too close, Alex thought. She had to end this quickly.

He was fast and he was gaining confidence. Plus, even though he didn't have any training and depended wholly on his weapon, if the small club made contact with her head she would be in trouble.

They circled each other and she realized that the man wasn't even glancing at Shepard. She now had his full attention and didn't know if that was the good news or the bad news.

She realized that he had been driving the fight and decided that she had to take charge and direct what happened next. Alex pretended to stumble on her left heel and he struck quickly, swinging the blackjack at her.

She pushed off with the same left heel and threw herself into the arc of his attack. This time, however, she raised her left forearm to block the blow before the swing was complete.

It was still a jarring blow, but it was his wrist and not the club that made contact—and that was the difference between a bruise and a broken arm.

While he was off balance, Alex launched a kick with her right foot while grabbing his wrist with her left hand. He grunted in surprise as she pulled the blackjack out of that hand and clocked him in the head with it.

He fell with a look of dumb shock still on his face. Alex turned him over and pulled out his wallet.

"Grab his I.D.," she said to Shepard, who did the same with the first attacker.

Half a minute later Shepard handed her the man's I.D., which she photographed and sent to Zeta for a background.

Meanwhile, Shepard had found both men's phones and used their thumbprints to unlock them.

He scrolled through the devices, a frown on his face.

Then the report came in from Zeta. She gave Shepard the highlights. "Petty crime. No connection to terror groups, kidnapping rings, or the government."

"Not just petty crime. Some of this stuff is rough," Shepard said.

"Well, maybe they'll think twice next time," she said.

"I think we can do better than that, if I can take a minute," Shepard said.

"We don't have much time. We're lucky no one has come by."

"This won't take long," Shepard said.

Alex stepped forward to take a lookout position. At the sound of rustling, Alex turned around to see Shepard removing one of the attacker's pants, and then his shoes. Then he repeated the operation on the second man.

"You taking their pants?" she said.

"It will give them more to explain when they're found," Shepard said as he tossed the pants and shoes into a trash bin.

"You'll want to turn around for this," he said. Alex did and she heard more rustling as Shepard removed their undershorts and tossed them as well.

"I wish we could hear their explanation," Alex said as they walked calmly and purposefully out of the alley.

"They could always tell the truth: a female tourist beat them unconscious and then some guy took their pants," Shepard said.

Alex laughed out loud at that one, as she felt the adrenaline from the fight slowly dissipating. She was impressed that Shepard had kept his cool. He was even making jokes.

When they were a good distance and a few turns away from the alley, Shepard pointed to a bench and they sat. He pulled out the phones, took out a screen cleaner, and wiped them for prints.

As part of Zeta, Shepard's prints would not appear on any database in the world, but it was better to be safe than sorry.

"Now what? We can't just turn them into the police," Alex said.

"I hadn't thought that far ahead," Shepard said.

Alex scanned the area. "How about that?" she said, pointing to a mailbox outside of a bank.

"Sure. If we drop them inside they'll probably find their way to the police."

Before Alex got up she realized why she was shaky. The heel on her right shoe was loose. Of course, that was the foot she'd used to kick the second attacker.

Pulling the shoe off, she saw it was a loss. Besides the heel, the scuffs were bad.

They were too expensive and very impractical, but even so, they were a nice pair of shoes and it was a shame to waste them.

"Call us a cab. Alex Jackson needs to go shopping," she said to Shepard.

CHAPTER EIGHT

The guards didn't bring Tunca back until the next day.

The man took one step into the cell and fell into the hands of Morgan and Conley. Morgan didn't dare make eye contact with the two guards. It wouldn't help anything for them to see how he felt about them.

As they helped him onto his bed, Morgan saw that Tunca wasn't just thin, he was emaciated.

Conley gave the journalist a quick exam while keeping him talking.

"No concussion. Nothing broken that I can see," Conley announced.

"Of course, they are very good at what they do," Morgan said.

The agents got some water into Tunca but he turned down food.

"He just wants to sleep," Conley said.

When Tunca was comfortable Morgan asked, "Do they want information?" Morgan said.

Conley had a quick exchange with Tunca and then said, "He told everything he knew in his articles."

"So this is just part of the punishment?" Morgan asked.

Conley didn't respond. He didn't have to.

After a minute Conley said, "I know everything you're thinking. In a few weeks we can just get the hell out of here."

It was true, Morgan thought, but what about Tunca and the tens of thousands of men and women across the country like him?

And what about the millions of people left in the country who knew that places like this awaited them if they stepped out of line…or told too much of the truth?

Suddenly a few more weeks seemed like a hell of a long time.

Less than an hour later the guards returned and Conley said, "Dan, you have a visitor. Your daughter is here."

That got Morgan's attention.

He got up and the guards brought him to the central hub, and then into a room with a long counter that was partitioned into ten individual cubbies. Each cubby had had two chairs with a glass partition in between them. The glass was high enough that visitors couldn't pass anything to the inmates but low enough that they could hear one another.

Morgan saw his daughter sitting in the cubicle on the far end. That was better; it meant other people on only one side of them. Of course, Morgan had no illusions about privacy here. Especially in a political prison such as this, they had to assume the administration was listening in on prisoners' conversations with visitors.

Alex was blonde and wearing a brightly colored dress. She was also heavily made up and appeared more like a minor wannabe celebrity than the intelligent, practical daughter he'd known for more than twenty years.

That's undercover work for you, he thought.

"Hi Daddy!" Alex said with a forced brightness in her voice.

"Hi Honey," he said, taking a seat.

"When are you coming home?" she asked.

"Soon, but aren't you early? I thought you were too busy to come right away," he said. The fact was that she wasn't due for weeks.

"I hated the idea of you all alone here," she said, taking in the room. "It's awful."

Though Alex *Jackson* may not have exactly been his daughter, on that they could agree.

"I don't want you exposed to this, sweetie," he said.

She ignored his comment and said, "Do you want Mommy to call anyone? Can't we just fix this?"

"We can. It's all a big mistake. I've got a great lawyer and he'll sort it all out in no time. Is everything okay at home?"

"Yes, but now Mommy and I have to do all the arrangements for my birthday party without you," she said with a pout.

"Like I said, it won't be long and I don't want you to worry," he said.

"I'll stay as long as it takes," she replied.

"Then try to have fun while you're here and stay out of trouble," he said.

As they filled out the rest of the visit with pleasantries, Morgan decoded what she'd told him so far: Everything was on track and she'd simply decided to set up the back office early.

All he had to do was sit tight and keep to the timetable.

The problem was that as they spoke he realized that something was wrong. Alex wasn't nervous. And she was doing an excellent job maintaining her cover. These weren't his agent's instincts kicking in; these were his father's instincts.

As they got up and said good-bye, Morgan realized what it was. Alex was wearing a cardigan over her dress.

A *long-sleeved* cardigan.

She was intentionally hiding something from him. An injury?

Had there been trouble? He was suddenly sure of it. And she'd just been here a few days. If they kept to the mission plan, they would all be here for more than another month.

And there would be plenty of opportunities for real trouble when the mission went into its active phase.

Suddenly his frustration with what was going on in this country and this prison threatened to boil over. On top of everything else, the longer the mission went on, the greater the danger to the back office personnel—the greater the danger to Alex.

He was sure she could handle anything they threw at her...and yet that pit in his stomach was growing by the second.

Heading back through the hub, Morgan passed a series of offices. There was a man in a suit talking to two subordinates, and suddenly the posture of the guards escorting him changed. They stood up straight, grasping him firmly.

Who was the man in the suit? The warden? Probably. Well if that was the case, Morgan thought he might like to file a few complaints...

The man turned around and Morgan got his first good look at him. He would have recognized him even without the eye patch.

Morgan put his head down. If the warden saw him, the operation would be over—and their carefully wrought escape plan would likely be worth nothing.

A few steps later they were past the warden and Morgan was out of immediate danger. However, this changed everything.

Of course, it should have been impossible. Zeta had checked the records of every guard and member of the staff—none of them had been working at any previous prison that Morgan or Conley had ever visited in Turkey.

But Morgan hadn't run into this man in a prison. And it would have been impossible for him to show up on any computer check.

Back in the cellblock, as he and the guards approached the cell, Conley could tell something was wrong.

Morgan knew Peter was thinking of their carefully wrought plan: They would soon be assigned to work in the prison laundry, where they would begin assembling equipment and resources for the escape. That would take weeks of careful work.

It was a solid plan. And they would have Zeta crawling around the prison's computer system to make sure it went off without a hitch.

It was a shame that they wouldn't be able to wait weeks. They needed a new plan, one that got them out of here very soon.

"Dan..." Conley said, when they were a few steps closer.

When the guard with the scar on his cheek grabbed his left shoulder to shove him into his cell Morgan was moving before he had consciously decided to do anything.

His arm swung around wide so that when Morgan's fist made contact with the guard's face it had quite a bit of force behind it.

The man stumbled back, gave Morgan an uncomprehending look, and then fell to the floor.

Well, Morgan thought, *he isn't so tough when the prisoners hit back.*

CHAPTER NINE

Boston, Massachusetts
Fifteen Years Ago

"Just be home before school starts," Jenny had said as he prepared to leave the house.

"If the job is more than two weeks I can just turn it down," Morgan replied. That would give him plenty of time, since there was a month before the start of school.

Jenny looked at him in silence before she kissed him good-bye.

That silence, more than anything else, made Morgan determined to be home as promised. Alex was starting second grade. He wasn't going to miss it.

For one, he didn't want to disappoint Jenny. And for another, he had missed too much already.

He was in a bit of a mood by the time he got to Conley's place and in even more of a mood when they reached the diner. Plante was waiting for them in a booth in the back.

Their handler was somewhere around thirty, with already thinning hair. He was wearing a polo shirt and slacks, appearing uncomfortable out of a suit. The fact that he had made the trip to Boston showed the partners that this was an important mission.

"Cobra, Cougar," Plante said, extending his hand.

Using their code names was another sign that this one was serious.

Once the handshaking and pleasantries were over, Morgan got right down to business.

"What's the target?" he asked.

Plante was used to his direct approach, so it didn't faze him. He simply said, "A general in the Turkish military, currently in charge of the Turkish forces on Cyprus," Plante said.

"Why is he a target?" Morgan said.

"You know you're not allowed to ask me that and I'm definitely not allowed to tell you. That's how this works. I give you the target, you do the job. Any other intel you get comes only if it's necessary for the operation. However, I can tell you this mission is of high international importance and impacts U.S. interests directly."

Morgan simply stared back at the man silently. Conley kept quiet as well. He had seen this game play out before.

After nearly a full minute, Plante sighed and said, "I could lose my job for this…General Ketenci is building a power base. He has long-standing family ties to the military and is very well connected politically. We think he has plans to stage a military coup and install himself as a dictator."

"What's the timeframe?" Morgan said.

"Five years maximum," Plante said.

"A lot can happen in five years," Morgan said.

"Yeah, and a lot of it bad. We have solid intelligence that he is personally planning to stage an incident in the next eighteen months that will allow him to invade the three quarters of the island of Cyprus that is currently under Greek control. As it is, he doesn't stay on his side of the line. He's been testing the Greeks for months."

Plante hesitated for a few seconds and then added, "And his troops don't behave when they are on Greek soil. They commit the standard robberies and assaults but there's something worse going on. Young women have begun to disappear. Very few are found. And none are found alive."

They'd take the job. Plante knew Morgan well and had carefully selected the details he revealed to push his buttons. And yet Morgan also knew the man wouldn't lie to them.

"The target's code name is Kang," Plante said.

He turned to Conley. "What do you think Peter?"

"Sounds like a bad guy," Conley said.

Two weeks later they were on a plane heading for Cyprus. They flew into Larnaca Airport, south of the "Green Line"—the raggedy east-west buffer that separated the Turkish North and the Greek Cypriot south.

Though the Turks held less than a third of the island, they had kept more than twenty thousand troops there since the 1974 invasion and occupation.

That number was less than the forty thousand they had used in the invasion. Even so, the Turkish garrison was now at least a third larger than the Greek forces.

Given the fact that the Turkish force estimates were notoriously inaccurate, the twenty thousand figure was probably low. The official public numbers were nonsense, of course. And even the CIA had trouble keeping an accurate count.

Whatever the number, the Greeks had plenty good reason to worry.

The lower numbers also gave European nations cover for their inaction about the growing threat.

The British had two military bases on the island. And the UN was patrolling the new buffer zone between the two sectors. And yet here Morgan and Peter were.

Plante liked to call the partners *specialists.* But at times like this Morgan knew what they really were: trash collectors.

And they *specialized* in the trash nobody wanted to touch.

Their visas listed the reason for their trip as business and pleasure. It allowed them to scout the business districts and the remote places where they could more easily cross the border undetected.

The U.N. troops patrolling the buffer zone made that a bit harder, but not much.

The agents rented a car and headed to their hotel in the capital, Nicosia. It was a beautiful city, with the Green Line running right down the middle. Not surprisingly, the buffer zone was the most heavily patrolled in the city.

Yet the agents were able to cross over and visit the Turkish quarter fairly easily. They chose the checkpoint in the center of Nicosia. The streets were quaint and medieval, with a number of modern restaurants, shops, and boutiques.

Morgan thought that Jenny would like it, until he got closer to the buffer zone and saw the concrete, razor wire, sandbags, and gun embankments.

It was ugly, certainly, but he knew it was also necessary. The wounds from the invasion had still not healed in the thirty years since, and a little distance would give the people on both sides time to figure out the next step. It would help keep the U.S. from getting dragged into a nightmare.

Morgan understood that these people would likely only get that time if Morgan and Conley did their jobs.

On the Turkish side, the buildings were roughly the same medieval stone structures—though there were more kebab shops than restaurants, and the signs were in Turkish instead of Greek.

But more importantly, this side of the line appeared to be lost in time. There were no modern storefronts, no trendy boutiques. If you took away the cars and the electric lights, Morgan imagined this side of the city hadn't changed much in a hundred years.

He wouldn't have said the north side was any worse, but it definitely felt less alive than the bustling south.

The partners had lunch close to the buffer zone so they could observe the soldiers, who were reasonably alert and guarded. Morgan wasn't surprised. There was still plenty of tension at the border, and both the guards and the customs people on both sides were on edge.

Of course, the crossings had been open less than two years. With any luck, people would relax and the soldiers could fall into the bored complacency that characterized most border duty in non-hostile countries.

These two countries could use a little boredom, he thought.

Their next stop was the "international" airport in Nicosia. No longer a working airport, it has been one of the main targets of the Turkish invasion in 1974. Overnight, it had gone from a brand new international hub to a literal graveyard, complete with rotting passenger jets sitting on the tarmac.

Because it was in the city and in the center of the buffer zone, the airport was relatively heavily patrolled.

However, the size of the grounds and the fact that it was mostly protected by loose chain link fencing meant that it would likely be the best place inside the city for an illicit evening border crossing.

The next day they were up early and in the car heading west. They took their time, surveying the various checkpoints, walls, and fencing. Wherever they went, the closer they got to the green zone, the more nervous the population got.

Morgan and Conley made their last stop at a small fishing village called Pomos, on the furthest west coast of the island. It had green mountains on one side, the Mediterranean on the other, and beaches in between.

"Maybe when we're done with this mess I might come back and stay here for a little while," Conley said.

They found a small inn to stay for the night and had dinner there. In the dining room, Morgan saw what appeared to be locals and a few other tourists.

The innkeeper and his wife, Kostas and Elena, were polite but guarded, though they perked up when they realized that Morgan and Conley were Americans. The partners spent a pleasant evening with the middle-aged couple talking about their teenage daughter, who would be getting back from a school trip with her friends to "the mainland."

When Peter asked the couple how they felt about living so close to the border Kostas shrugged and said, "It's okay. There's been some trouble with the soldiers, but not here."

Morgan and Conley turned in early and headed to their rooms. It was less than an hour later that they heard the screams. Conley was already in the hallway when Morgan got there.

Morgan felt the comforting weight of his Walther in his shoulder holster. He had no doubt that Conley had his .45 under his jacket.

"We have to be careful Dan. We can't let this get out of hand," Conley said.

"I'm always careful," Morgan replied.

Downstairs, he saw that there were two guests in a small den. They seemed both scared and confused. Elena showed up, calling out in Greek. There was another scream from out back and then recognition on Elena's face. "Maria!" she cried.

That was her daughter's name.

Morgan had his gun out and showed it to her. "Elena, we're going to help you. Get Kostas and turn on whatever lights you have outside. Keep everybody inside and together."

"Maria..." she said, sounding desperate.

"We'll find her," Morgan said. Just then Kostas showed up carrying a shotgun. He seemed comfortable with it but Morgan didn't want civilians running around getting themselves or anyone else hurt.

"Stay inside," Conley said. "Let us help."

Morgan and Conley raced out the back and into a Turkish army fire team.

There were four men in military uniforms. Two of them held rifles on the agents while two other men each held a struggling teenage girl in their arms.

The uniforms gave them away. These weren't just soldiers out making trouble. They were making a statement. They were telling the Greek people that they weren't safe, that the Turkish army could come and go at will and do what they wanted. It sent a message of powerlessness to the Greek Cypriots and created a sense of invulnerability around the Turkish army.

It was exactly the kind of demoralizing psychological op you would run if you were preparing a population for invasion.

Morgan and Conley each took aim at one of the soldiers with rifles who, in turn, took aim at them.

The soldiers were all screaming in Turkish. Morgan didn't need Conley's understanding of the language to know they were telling the agents to put their guns down.

It was a classic Mexican standoff with the additional element of two teenage hostages.

"Hold on!" Morgan shouted. "We can talk about this."

That was met with just more shouting in Turkish. This was going nowhere, and the longer it went on the greater the chance that something would go wrong.

Morgan shot a sidelong glance at Conley and said, "My friend and I are going to shoot you. We won't kill you but it's going to hurt."

Then, together, Morgan and Conley each took aim at the left shoulder of the men holding the rifles. Shooting their right shoulder would have increased the chance of a twitch in their right hand, each of which was poised on the trigger of a rifle.

Both shots hit their marks and the men recoiled, dropping their weapons without firing them. As a bonus, one of the men holding the girls let go of her as he fumbled for his own weapon.

To her credit, the girl kept to her feet and immediately leapt toward the house.

Morgan didn't hesitate, as soon as the girl was clear he clipped the one who had been holding her in the shoulder.

By the time he fell to the ground, the girl was safely inside.

"Get them out of here," Morgan said to Conley. He trained his gun on the last soldier, who was holding a girl of about fifteen with dark curly hair. She was scared but keeping it together even though the soldier now had a combat knife to her throat.

Conley made sure the injured soldiers weren't holding any weapons and ushered them into the night and toward the border.

"Maria!" Elena said. Morgan could hear a mother's panic in her voice.

"Tell them to stay back," the soldier said in broken English.

Morgan spared a glance and saw that Kostas was there as well, holding the shotgun but not wanting to point it in his daughter's direction.

"Put the gun down Kostas," Morgan said.

"You are American," the soldier said. "I don't like Americans."

"I'm reserving judgment on your people but I definitely don't like you," Morgan said. "Release the girl and I'll let you live."

The soldier turned his body, keeping Maria squarely between himself and Morgan. Then he pressed the point of the knife harder into her neck. Not deep enough to kill her but deep enough to break the skin.

Maria called out and her mother gave another scream.

"I am leaving. I am also taking the girl with me. If you follow, I will kill her instantly," he said.

"I can't let you do that," Morgan said.

"You cannot stop me, if you try she dies here," the soldier said. He spat at the ground. "You Americans, you think you can come to our country and make rules. We make the rules. And tonight, *I* make the rules." He pressed the knife against the girl's neck, deep enough this time to draw blood.

Morgan had no choice; he put down his Walther and showed his hands.

Then he took a step forward and said, "Two things: This isn't your country. And second, *orospu çocuğu.*"

It was one of the few phrases he knew in Turkish. It might not have been fair to the soldier's mother, but it had the desired effect.

The soldier tossed the girl to the side and charged Morgan with his knife. He was big, at least three inches taller than Morgan himself.

The Turk telegraphed his knife thrust, giving Morgan time to deflect it with his right forearm. This put Morgan on the "outside" of the attacker's body. It also allowed him to hook his fingers and tear into the man's face.

"If you control the head, you control the fight," one of his instructors at *The Farm* had taught him.

Bad guys are useless without their heads, he and Conley used to joke.

And also without two good eyes, Morgan saw.

The soldier had dropped his knife and was clutching the mess that was his left eye. He howled.

Morgan grabbed the man by one shoulder and shook him. "I've taken your eye, but I'm going to let you live. Go back with your *dangalak* friends."

Conley appeared from the night and said, "You don't have to just learn the insults."

Morgan turned and saw Kostas and Elena huddled over their daughter.

"They're gone," Conley said.

The family looked up and then stood. Elena gave the men a pained smile and led her daughter inside.

Kostas choked out a *thank you* and then said, "Who are you? Are you policemen?"

Morgan shook his head. "No we're not policemen. Would you believe we're trash collectors?"

Conley stepped in and said, "Kostas, we can't stay. It's better if we're not here for the police."

The man nodded and thanked them again.

"Go see your wife and daughter. Those men won't be back," Morgan said.

As the agents headed up to their rooms Conley asked, "What did you do to that last soldier?"

"He'll live but he'll have terrible depth perception," Morgan said.

"At least we didn't have to kill any of them," Conley said.

It was true, as much as Morgan had wanted to. They couldn't afford a flare-up here, with possible reprisals and further attacks. They still had a target and a mission.

Conley flipped open his phone and called Plante to tell their handler he might have to handle the local police.

When he closed the phone he said, "We have movement and a possible location on the target tomorrow. We should stop back at Nicosia, pick up our gear and head east."

CHAPTER TEN

Cyprus
Fifteen Years Ago

Famagusta was on the far eastern edge of the buffer zone. Morgan drove while Conley talked on the cell phone with Plante. It took a few hours to drive there, with a stop at their hotel in Nicosia to get their gear.

The general was planning something. There had been suspicious troop movements, as well as the movement of some heavy equipment. It could be the early stages of an invasion, or some sort of reconstruction of Famagusta.

The second option wouldn't be much better than an attack, considering how bitterly the town was contested. Morgan's money was on military action. The analysts at Langley were convinced that an invasion was imminent. And Morgan had seen enough of the intel himself to believe it.

The agents had less than an hour of darkness left by the time they parked the car. They grabbed their duffel bags and walked to the beach, which was in Greek territory. Low fencing separated it from the Turkish section.

On the plus side, the Greeks still had the beach. On the other hand, the beach gave them an excellent view of what they'd lost.

Famagusta was another graveyard, but in some ways it was much worse than the airport.

Transportation hubs were among the first targets in any invasion. They were simply a casualty of war. The empty airport and rusting aircraft were a symbol of the struggle between two powers.

Famagusta was different. It was a small city where 40,000 Greeks had lived and worked literally on the beach. During the Turkish airstrikes, those forty thousand had fled with nothing but the clothes on their backs.

What they left was not an unfortunate but normal by-product of military conflict. Here the ghosts weren't planes and airport facilities.

In Famagusta, the ghosts were beachfront high-rise hotels and apartment buildings, as well as street after street of homes, shops, and restaurants that had been abandoned for forty years. This wasn't transportation hardware or infrastructure; this was people's lives.

Now the town was on the Turkish side of the border, fenced off and slowly decaying. The fencing was shoddy, four or five feet of a mix of chain link, corrugated metal, and plastic netting.

It was easy enough to avoid the Turkish army lookout. They simply ducked under the fencing until they were out of the line-of-sight and found their spot. Morgan tossed his duffel bag over the fence and followed it, with Conley right behind him.

With twenty minutes until dawn they hurried to the hotel that Conley had chosen based on the general's expected route.

Officially, the general would be making an inspection tour. He would be traveling with only half a dozen soldiers and—if their intelligence was good—would be outside and vulnerable for quite some time.

Morgan and Conley found the first hotel and headed up to the fifth floor. It was just a couple of blocks from the beach. They found a broken window that had a good line-of-sight to the avenue below. They planted some light charges and a few other surprises, and then headed downstairs. Outside, they headed to the hotel across the street.

It was getting light outside as they found a fourth floor spot to wait.

There were a lot of variables here. The intelligence was new—if it was accurate, they were in business. If not, it was back to the drawing board.

Normally, Morgan preferred plenty of time to plan an operation. And they just hadn't had time given how late this new intelligence had come in.

Within two hours, they had movement. Conley checked with Plante, who gave them a fire-at-will authorization.

They could see soldiers in the distance. Morgan scanned them through his binoculars as Conley took position behind his sniper rifle.

"Five total," Morgan said.

"I have them," Conley replied.

"I see a general's uniform," Morgan said.

"I see it," Conley said. Then he added, "Kang's identity is confirmed, it's General Ketenci."

Morgan quickly got into position behind his own sniper rifle. He found the men in his scope and chose his targets.

"Ready," Morgan said.

"I have him," Conley said. "On three….two…one."

Conley fired at the general while Morgan fired at his first target, the soldier to the general's immediate right. Without waiting, he swung the rifle and fired again. Each of Morgan's shots hit the soldiers in the shoulder.

He had no doubt that Conley had hit the general center mass and that it was a kill shot. But Morgan was only aiming to injure, and both men went down—as did, of course, the general. The injured men were out of the fight and would distract the remaining soldiers.

The two uninjured soldiers reacted with admirable speed and drew their weapons, scanning the buildings around them, searching for the source of the gunshots.

And that's when Conley pulled out the remote and set off the first of the charges in the room across the street. There were flashes of light and even a bit of smoke to complete the illusion.

The men were well-trained and fired at the window as Morgan and Conley threw their weapons into their duffel bags.

With their equipment secure, Morgan checked on the soldiers. They were dragging their injured friends and dead leader to cover.

Conley hit another two charges and the soldiers moved faster, dragging the three men the last few feet into a building.

Morgan and Conley didn't wait anymore, they sprinted down the stairs. Their simple trick would only work if they got out of the building and the area before it was swarming with Turkish soldiers.

They took the stairs at a run and hit the east exit of the hotel. They kept running until they had put a few blocks between them and the general's team. Morgan could hear commotion behind them as they cut toward the fence. In another two blocks they were there. They found a section of chain link that was nearly falling down and simply stepped over it. Then they hopped down from the short cinder block wall and were standing on the beach.

They were now safely on the Greek side…with four older Greek men staring at them.

Without hesitating, Conley glanced over his shoulder, shouted something in Greek, and made a hand gesture at the Turkish side: he opened his hand, splayed the fingers and shoved it, palm out, toward the occupied territory.

The Greek men nodded approvingly and then mimicked the gesture.

That done, the agents didn't tarry. They headed down the beach and back to their car. They kept their pace to a casual stroll to keep from drawing attention to themselves.

Morgan allowed himself to relax a bit when they reached the car. It was surprisingly quiet around them. Whatever commotion there was in the occupied city, he couldn't hear it over the morning din of activity around them.

They headed back to the hotel and stowed their gear in the room. They called Plante, to confirm that they had completed the mission, and then made sure they were seen having breakfast at the hotel café.

Morgan realized he was tired. It had been a long night and the adrenalin that had kept him going from the fight at the inn until now was wearing off. The smart thing to do was to sleep before they left, but Morgan found that he didn't want to wait.

"I'm heading to the airport," he said.

"I'll go with you," Conley said.

"I thought you were going to make another visit to the west coast, hit those beaches."

"This place has lost its allure for me," Conley said. "Maybe I'll come back another time."

Morgan understood. Then he decided to bring up a subject that he and Conley very rarely discussed.

"Do you think it will do any good?" Morgan asked.

"One less bad guy, who was on his way to being a *very* bad guy with a lot of power. Yeah, I think it will do some good. It won't fix much over here. And we'll see about Turkey, but I think things will be a little better."

"We did take out the trash, but that's the problem with garbage. As soon as you take it out, it starts piling up again," Morgan said.

CHAPTER ELEVEN

Erdoğan Prison, Present day

The guards hadn't beaten Morgan too badly before they tossed him into one of the yellow rooms. He suspected their restraint was because if they injured him, he might end up in the infirmary and miss out on solitary, which was the real punishment.

He saw why they called these 'sponge cells.' They were padded with yellow foam mattresses. Theoretically, the foam made it harder for prisoners to injure themselves if the isolation got to them.

That was a real danger, and Morgan knew it from experience. He'd developed his own ways of dealing with that kind of isolation but he'd seen tough men crack in a relatively short time.

He hoped Dr. Erdem was holding out.

Hitting a guard would get him at least a week in solitary, if not more. But Morgan knew that this time, he wasn't going to need any of his strategies for coping with isolation.

Because this time he wouldn't be staying.

The door was solid and it had opened with a key card. If he was on the other side of the door and had all day, he couldn't break *into* the room without a card. On this side, it would be even tougher.

Fortunately, he had a guy.

Morgan focused on the lone security camera in one corner of the room. It covered almost the entire cell. The only way to avoid its gaze was to stand straight under it in the very corner.

It was not something your average prisoner could do for long, especially since it wouldn't get you anything except a few minutes of privacy.

Fortunately, a few minutes of privacy was all Morgan needed.

He stood in the corner and reached straight up to the camera. He grabbed the housing and snapped it off on one side. He brought it down and found what he wanted, two small metal discs exactly the same size as a hearing aid battery.

He popped them out and quickly replaced the camera cover.

The discs replaced the batteries in his "hearing aids," adding some clever electronics. The new batteries not only lasted much longer than the ordinary ones, but they also transformed the more or less standard heading aids into full-featured Zeta ear comms.

These were only one of the many surprises that Zeta had built into President Shakir's new prison system through multiple contractors operating under international shell corporations.

Using the security cameras had been a nice touch. Ironically, security equipment got even less scrutiny than other materials that went into constructing a prison. All a Zeta agent had to do was get himself thrown into solitary and he'd have access to the tech.

Morgan thought about some of the other goodies that Shepard's division had built into the equipment that now sat in the prison laundry. It really was a remarkable and elegant plan. Morgan was almost sorry that he and Conley wouldn't be able to execute it.

Morgan hit the switch on one of the devices. "Cobra here. You there Shepard?"

* * * *

"Cobra?" Shepard said into his phone with more than a little surprise in his voice. Alex put down her coffee and headed over, signaling Shepard to put her dad on speaker.

"How are you calling us?" Shepard said.

"I'm in solitary," Morgan said.

"That's a little early," Alex said. She had to force herself to add, "Cobra."

"Change of plans," her father's voice said.

Shepard looked stricken. "Um, there's no changing this plan. The schedule is essential—"

"Okay, so it's a whole new plan," her father said irritably. "My cover was nearly blown. I recognized the warden. We have history." Then before Shepard could speak, he added, "Wasn't your fault. His name wouldn't have kicked up on any search. He was military; it was fifteen years ago, and I never even knew his name. But if he sees me…"

"I take it you didn't part on good terms?" Alex said.

"His men were injured. And he lost an eye—he blames me," her father said, his voice remarkably calm.

"I'm sure it's just a misunderstanding," Alex said.

"Oh, not at all, and he'll want to kill me if he sees me. Plus, he'll figure out pretty quick that I'm an agent of some kind," Morgan said.

"So we'll have to abort and get you out of there," Alex said.

"I don't want to leave without Dr. Erdem. We may not get another chance," Morgan said.

"We'd need weeks to come up with a new operation," Shepard said. "And it sounds like you may not have *days.*"

"Cougar and I are prepared to work quickly," he replied.

"Would you care to share this remarkable new plan with us?" Alex asked.

"We're working on the details. We'll firm them up when I get back up in the general population. For now, can you get me into Erdem's room? Then I need you to arrange his release back upstairs."

"What about you?" Alex asked.

"Give me a day in here to make it look good and then do the same."

"We have nearly complete control of the prison computer system. I can place the orders, but any check or audit will show breaks in protocol. You might only have a few days, maybe less, and that's if your one-eyed friend doesn't recognize you."

"Your new escape plan must really be something. We can't wait to hear the details," Alex said.

"Me too," her father said, with a hint of humor in his voice.

"The door will open in a few seconds," Shepard said.

"There it is," Morgan replied.

"Go outside and check for another open door. That will be Erdem's cell. Don't worry about the security cameras, I'll adjust the feeds."

"Thanks Shep, I'll report when I get topside. Cobra out."

Alex and Shepard gave each other a look.

"What just happened?" the young man asked.

* * * *

Morgan found Dr. Erdem lying on the ground, facing the wall. The cell was cool and there was no furniture other than a toilet—no bed or mattress.

Of course, the floor was padded, so that was something.

“Dr. Erdem,” Morgan said.

The man slowly turned and saw Morgan standing over him in civilian clothing. The scientist was in his mid-thirties and in reasonably good physical condition. “Are you okay, Dr. Erdem?” he asked.

The scientist got to his feet and Morgan could see that he was alert, much sharper than Morgan would have expected after so long in solitary.

“You're American,” Erdem said.

“I am. I've also come to help you. To get you out of here, but I'll need your help to do it,” he said.

“You don't seem like a lawyer,” Erdem said.

“It's not that kind of help,” Morgan said.

“State department? CIA? They threw me in here because they said I was a CIA spy. Are you here to trick me? To get me to agree to something so they can accuse me of whatever they want?”

“Frankly, Dr. Erdem, I don't see that your situation could get much worse. However, I've been authorized to tell you that your wife says the dog won't stop getting into the garbage since you left,” Morgan said.

Genuine surprise registered on Erdem's face. Then it took him several seconds to compose himself. “Okay, what's going on?” Erdem asked.

“I'm part of a private organization that provides assistance to the U.S. Government from time to time. My organization has been asked get you an…unofficial release,” Morgan said.

Erdem sized him up and said, “You mean some sort of an escape?”

“Yes, but my partner and I have run into a snag. We've had to accelerate the timeline.”

“Will this be dangerous?” Erdem asked.

“Almost certainly,” Morgan said.

“I see. I assume this will be my only chance?”

“Yes.”

“What do I do?”

“Right now, just follow the guards who will come later. You're going to be released back into your cell upstairs. After that, we'll have to act quickly and I will contact you when it's time.”

"What do I call you?"

"You can call me Dan," Morgan replied.

"Okay Dan, it appears I only have one option," Erdem said. Then the man added, "Is that some Boston I hear in your voice?"

"It is. Your file says you grew up in New York, until you headed to NASA."

"I'm Queens," he said. Then he added "Go Yankees," almost reflexively.

Silence hung in the air between them.

"Ah, I see. You're a Red Sox man. Is that a deal breaker?" Erdem said seriously.

Morgan waited a few seconds before answering. "We're trained to look past things like that. I'll do my job. Plus, I don't want to add to your problems,

considering the fact that you weren't able to sign a single decent free agent during the break and your bull pen might as well be a geriatric ward."

With that, Morgan stepped out of the cell, closed the door and headed back to his own cell.

CHAPTER TWELVE

"They let you out early," Conley said as the guards shoved Morgan back into his cell.

"Place was a dump. Didn't even have turn down service," Morgan said.

Tunca was sitting at on his bed, reading. He lowered the book and greeted Morgan with a nod.

"How's he doing?" Morgan said.

"A little sore but okay," Conley said.

Then Morgan tossed Conley one of the ear comms.

"It's operational now. I've been talking to Shep and Alex," Morgan said.

"I see that Dr. Erdem is back in his cell. What's going on?"

"I recognized the warden, though he didn't see me…yet. He was one of the soldiers from Cyprus. The leader of that merry band."

"We have to assume he'll recognize you and that he's still pissed about the eye," Conley said. "Bloch will want us to abort."

"Unless we come up with a better option. And do it pretty quick," Morgan said.

"The last plan took months to put together. It also had the advantage of being quiet. We would have just disappeared. By the time they realized we were gone and figured it all out we would have been home."

"Our new schedule may require us to make a little more noise," Morgan said.

"You don't say," Conley said.

"I'm thinking a prison riot," Morgan said.

"With this bunch?" Conley said, gesturing outside the cell.

That was a concern. The prisoners in this facility were not the rioting type. Students and journalists weren't the violent, hardened criminals that usually led prison riots. Even if they did riot, the administration would have little trouble putting it down. That was why Zeta had rejected the riot scenario right off the bat.

"I've got a twist and I think I've got a way to make it work. But first we need to figure out some details. Can you ask Tunca if he'd like to leave?"

"You think?"

"He's a native Turkish speaker. He might come in handy. Plus, I say we help him make the energy minister's deals with terrorists front-page news. That is, if you think we can trust him."

It wasn't a simple question. Even if Tunca had nothing but hatred for his captors, there was no guarantee he wouldn't use information to try to make a deal with them.

They would be betting the entire operation on a man they barely knew. Conley had been speaking to him and Morgan trusted his partner's judgment.

"We can trust him," Conley said.

"Okay, let's get to work," Morgan said.

* * * *

When Diana Bloch looked up, she saw Mr. Smith entering her office. He hadn't called to tell her he was coming, or to give her a chance to prepare a report, or a briefing.

That told her that this was serious. And that he wanted nothing but straight unrehearsed answers from her.

Somewhere in his sixties, with his trademark tailored suit and neatly combed white hair, he appeared to be a CEO or hedge fund manager. Of course, in his life, Bloch knew that he may have likely been both of those.

He still was, in a way. If Diana functioned as a managing director of Zeta Division, he was the CEO—as well as a member of the board of the parent company, the Aegis Initiative.

He was also her boss. Or one of them. Of course, he was the only one of her supervisors she had actually met. The other members of that exclusive international club were even more private than Mr. Smith.

"Hello, Diana," he said, extending his hand.

She shook it. "Sir."

He gestured to her chair and said, "Please take a seat."

He sat in the guest chair as she took her own place. Normally, that would put her in a position of power, but she had no illusions about who was in charge here.

"I understand there has been a complication in the mission in Turkey," Mr. Smith said.

"Yes, we're exploring other options. Normally I'd simply extract my agents but Cobra and Cougar want a little time to develop an alternative solution to our problem," Diana said.

"Let them," Mr. Smith said.

"Excuse me?" Diana said. It wasn't a surprise that those two wanted to try to improvise a new mission plan when the last one took months to put together and years of groundwork, but Smith was much less…impulsive.

"We need Dr. Erdem extracted right away," Mr. Smith said.

"My agents…"

"Know what they are doing. And they know the risks," he said.

"What's going on?" Diana said.

"Dr. Erdem's work is very important to the space program, as you know. But his nuclear power system is very important to the United States' new space-based weapons platform. We need that system, right away," Mr. Smith said.

"I understand that. But I have two agents' lives to consider," Diana said. "And I'm trying to make sure we don't burn the assets we've carefully put in place in the construction of the new Turkish prison system."

"All important, but we need that scientist. And not to put too fine a point on it but President Shakir *can't have him.* And I don't mean we don't want Shakir to have him, but we absolutely can't allow his expertise to fall into the hands of a man like that."

"Or what—Dr. Erdem will be eliminated?"

"Even if the United States didn't do it, there are a half a dozen intelligence agencies who would. His lifespan would be measured in weeks. There are too many weapons applications to his work. And there are too many things that he can build that Shakir can never be allowed to have."

"I see," Diana said.

"How much confidence do you have in your agents?" Mr. Smith said.

"If anyone can do it," Diana said.

"Then let's hope they can," Mr. Smith.

* * * *

After her conversation with her dad, Alex thought she was done being surprised for the day.

And then she spoke to Diana Bloch.

"What did she say? What are we authorized for?" Shepard asked.

"Whatever you need. She told me that you are authorized to do whatever you have to do to get them out. Whatever happens, Aegis wants the scientist. These orders come from Mr. Smith himself."

Alex could see Shepard wrestling with that information. Usually, on field missions they were howling for resources and authorizations. Here they had a blank check.

"What about covering our tracks?" Shepard asked.

"If you can, but the mission comes first," Alex said.

"Wow," Shepard said.

Alex felt the same way. Zeta had spent years building back doors into the prison computer system, and planting tech throughout the prisons during their construction.

If President Shakir learned about any of that, they risked burning assets that could never be replaced. She figured Dr. Erdem must be very important.

"I can try to hide what we're doing a bit. I can cover some of our work with strategic system crashes. And there are some other tricks," Shepard said.

"As long as it doesn't compromise the mission," Alex said. "We need to get them all out."

"I understand, but if your father ends up back in a Turkish prison in a year or two, I want to make sure we can get him out then too," Shepard said.

"Fair enough," Alex said. The fact was that Zeta agents as well as any number of American citizens or allies could easily end up guests of President Shakir in the near future.

"What do you need?" she said.

"I'll talk to O'Neal. I can run it from here, but we'll need the whole tech division on this," he said.

"In the meantime, I'll sort out some emergency transport options," Alex said.

That was going to be tricky since they had no time and no details—because they would be making it up as they went along.

So all she had to do was figure out exactly how it all would end and develop a plan to have transportation waiting at the right place and time, and then develop an exfiltration plan from a country that would very likely be a hot zone for them before they were finished.

Alex ordered up some fresh coffee and they both got to work.

CHAPTER THIRTEEN

"Dr. Erdem, this is Tunca Guler," Conley said, when all four men were in the courtyard after lunch.

Tunca and Erdem conversed in Turkish and then Morgan said, "We have to leave, and very soon. Once we make the call this is going to happen very quickly."

"We need to know you are both prepared," Morgan said. Conley quickly translated for Tunca.

"We had a very low risk scenario but we have had to abandon it. This could get tricky," Conley said.

Tunca asked a question and Morgan didn't need to know Turkish to understand it. "The warden and I have history. If he sees me the operation is over; this is our only chance to get you out," Morgan said.

"The warden and I also have some history," Erdem said. "He hopes to take credit for convincing me to serve President Shakir. His methods have been...crude. What will happen to him if we are successful?"

"I imagine it won't be good," Conley said.

"Well, I find that staying here is risky. And I would like to see my wife and children again. If it hurts the warden that is just a plus," Erdem said.

"Tunca is with us as well," Conley said.

"Then let's make the call," Morgan said, hitting the button on his ear comm as Conley did the same.

"Cobra here," Morgan said.

Alex and Shepard came on the line with the two agents.

"What's your status?" Alex said.

"We're ready. Dr. Erdem is with us now. And we're taking a journalist named Tunca Guler."

"It's not like one more will upset our careful planning," Alex said.

"He's a native speaker, he'll be a great asset," Conley said.

"What have you got for us, Alex?" Morgan said.

"Complete access to the prison computers. We can control doors and make sure the heavy weapons stay locked up in any riot scenario," Shepard said.

"Keep them locked up but, for now, I'd like to focus on causing a riot in our sister prison," Morgan said.

"What?" Shepard said.

"Can you do it?" Morgan asked.

"Misdirection…" Alex said.

"Exactly. We want a real emergency at Izmir Prison. Can you keep them jumping?"

"I can do more than that," Shepard said. "My riot plan for your prison will work even better there. Even as it starts to go to hell, we can alter the feeds so that their security cameras show normal."

"There is one problem, there are also women and children at Izmir prison," Alex said.

"Can you keep them locked away for the duration?" Morgan asked.

"Yes," Shepard replied. "And I can make sure all the weapons stay locked up."

"Protocol will have them send over some of the guards from here to provide support. That will give us fewer to deal with," Conley added.

"I can make sure those orders go through and see if I can transfer your prison's riot response team as soon as the party starts," Shepard said.

"How soon can we get it started?" Morgan asked. "I'd like to get out of here before dinner. It's slop night again."

"We don't have a plan to get you out of the prison. We have no ground transport through the city, and no exfiltration plan to get you out of Turkey. We can get started, but…"

"Start immediately," Morgan said.

"Even a few days," Alex began.

"No, now that our original plan has been blown, there's no value in sticking around any longer than necessary. Erdem or I could get thrown back into solitary. The warden could see me. And that's just the obvious stuff that could go wrong. If we're going to do this, the longer we wait, the lower the chance of success. Alex, Shep, don't try to figure it all out at once. Get it started, we'll do our part, and we'll figure out the rest as we go."

"Wait," Conley said as he shut off his comm and spoke quickly to Tunca and Erdem in Turkish. "What are you thinking for ground transport once we get out of here?" he said when he came back on.

"Something civilian. We'll stay away from city buses or any official vehicles in case they can be tracked. I was thinking a tour bus, something that will be ignored."

"Good idea. It's a solid protocol but Tunca points out that tourists, particularly Americans, are suspect now. Apparently, if we really want to be ignored we have to pose as Kurds."

"Kurds?" Shep said.

"They are a...disfavored minority. Routinely ignored when they are not being harassed. In any sort of emergency situation they will not even register."

"Okay," Alex said. "I'll see what we can do with that, though I'm not sure you will pass for Kurds. Wait for our signal. When it starts it's going to happen fast."

* * * *

Thirty minutes later, Shepard looked away from his laptops.

Alex heard, "Shepard out," and then he turned to her and said, "We're ready. Say the word and I can turn the water off in the northeast section of the city."

"The water?" she asked.

"It will divert their attention there. Then we'll start with the fire alarms—and some rolling blackouts," he said. "While the police and city government are chasing those shadows we can start our operation at Izmir prison."

"Do it," Alex said.

Shep barked into his comm and hit something on the computer, then said, "Done."

CHAPTER FOURTEEN

Morgan could hear sirens in the city. From what Alex had told them it would soon be chaos out there. It certainly sounded like they had made a good start on it.

"Bad news," Alex's voice came on in his ear. "I'm afraid all four of you have Crimean-Congo hemorrhagic fever."

"Is it serious?" Morgan asked.

"You're pre-symptomatic right now, but symptoms may include internal bleeding, shock, and organ failure," Alex said cheerfully.

"What's the treatment?" Conley chimed in.

"We put an order in to have you moved to the infirmary where you will be quarantined," Alex said. "They should come for you any minute. This will get you out of the cellblock. We'll have more options when you are in the administrative hub. If nothing else, that's where the exit is."

The sirens were getting louder. There was also much more movement among the guards, who were now coming and going from the yard.

"Are things heating up in the Izmir prison?" Morgan asked.

"Quite a bit actually. Because of a remarkable series of computer crashes and errors, the guards are almost all locked up in various sealed sections, and the prisoners are in control of about half the prison."

The guards outside started shouting at the prisoners that they were going back to their cells early. Everyone filed into the cellblock and two guards Morgan didn't know were waiting for them outside their cell.

The guards were wearing surgical masks and shouting at them. "Apparently we're going to the infirmary," Conley said.

They picked up Erdem at his cell and the four prisoners were marched toward the hub. By now there was real tension in the air, and guards were rushing around.

They crossed the barred doors that led to the administrative area. After taking a few turns, they reached the infirmary where they were rushed into a long room with six beds. Morgan assumed it was a quarantine ward.

The guards left and they were locked in.

"That's progress I guess," Conley said.

"It's a bigger room, nicer beds," Morgan agreed.

And then the lights went out, and then came back on.

Morgan tapped on his ear comm and said, "We're in quarantine. And the lights just flickered."

"Yeah, that's Shep testing the system. Turns out they're also about to have difficulty with their computers," Alex said.

"I think we have an exit strategy. At least a start on one. We've put in an order to move all available medical personnel to Izmir prison. Let's get you in scrubs and lab coats. Cougar, I'll talk you through getting to the store room."

The door beeped and unlocked itself. Ten long minutes later, Conley reappeared carrying a pile of clothing.

He handed Morgan, Erdem, and Tunca scrubs. He'd even procured identification tags that clipped onto the front pockets. None of the pictures matched, of course, but from a distance they would be convincing.

Conley and Erdem put on their own scrubs and then threw lab coats over them.

"Why do you two get to be doctors?" Morgan demanded.

"Because we speak Turkish," Conley said. "We won't give ourselves away the second we open our mouths."

"And, as a point of fact, I am actually a doctor," Erdem added.

Alex chimed in over the comm. "Still working on the medical transfer orders, but I can get you to the armory while we sort that out," Alex said.

"Now you're talking," Morgan said.

Alex told them to wait. They heard some sort of alarm down the hall and then Alex said, "Go."

The hallway was clear. They left the quarantine area and turned into the general medical section.

The scrubs were a good disguise. Medical personnel would have more access throughout the prison. However, in the infirmary area itself, where everyone presumably knew each other, they wouldn't fool anyone for long.

They moved slowly and as quietly as they could, reaching the outer offices less than a minute later. A nurse called out to them. They rushed past her and she screamed after them.

"We've been made," Morgan said. "Run."

The four men rushed toward the medical wing door, which was very solid and very strong. By now, there was a fair amount of commotion behind them.

"Alex, the door…" Morgan said.

"Shep is on it," she said.

Over his shoulder, Morgan saw two actual doctors and two large orderlies approaching them. Conley yelled something in Turkish and the real medical personnel were now screaming at them and racing forward.

"Got it," Alex said.

There was a click inside the door and Morgan tried it. It opened, and he quickly ushered the others outside. The four Turks were almost on them when Morgan slipped out himself and slammed the door shut behind him.

He heard it lock. Then there was pounding on the other side.

"Can they get out?" Morgan asked.

"They'll be in there until Shepard lets them out," Alex said. "He's also cut off the phone system in that wing. Of course, there's nothing we can do about personal cell phones."

That was unfortunate, but it was just a matter of time until word got out that something was going on in the prison.

If the medical staff was alerted, their medical transfer idea was going to get tricky.

"Get us to the armory. We may have to fight our way out," Morgan said.

* * * *

Shepard was stricken. "Someone just tried to sound the general alarm," he said. "One of the doctors must have gotten through to someone. I've shut down the alarm system as well as power to the two-way radio hub."

Alex looked at Shepard, hoping for an answer, some sign that he had a technical solution for a situation that appeared to be quickly getting out of control.

Weapons seemed like a pretty good idea about now.

"You're clear to administration. The armory is—"

"We know where it is, just let us know if anyone is going to get in our way," Morgan said.

"We'll get you out of there, don't worry," Alex said.

"It's not all up to you. We had a good plan, it just got compromised. At a certain point, when it all goes to hell you have to embrace the chaos. You'll know when that is."

"I've got another attempt to sound the alarm," Shepard said.

This was getting bad.

If anyone sounded the general alarm, their options would get pretty limited, fast.

"I'm also getting a lot of movement in the central hub. There are just too many people in there, too many guards," Shepard said.

That was bad—her father and the others had to be free to move as they all came up with a way out. And movement would be nearly impossible if the administration section was filled with guards.

"Cobra, Cougar stay put. Too much activity around you," Shepard said.

Alex studied the security camera feeds on one of Shepard's screens. Too many men walking around with too much urgency.

"Can you give me a guard-down alert, put it at the end of cellblock B," Alex said.

"Sure," Shepard replied, tapping at his keyboard. The alert would get other guards running but not make them break out the heavy weapons and riot gear. Alex saw movement but there were still too many people around.

"Give me another one, cell block A," she said.

The process played out again, with more guards running to that scene.

"Keep things open for now, but if they head back to the hub, lock them in the cellblock," Alex said.

Once that happened there would be no going back. With prison personnel locked out of the hub, there would be no hiding what was going on.

Alex only hoped her father and the others got out before that happened.

CHAPTER FIFTEEN

Morgan could hear what he recognized as one of the lower priority alarms, either a guard down, or a fight. It was a good move and would divert prison manpower without sounding the general alarm.

Now, if they could just get to the weapons they could shoot their way out of the administration hub if they had to.

Of course, they still had two hundred yards of driveway and courtyard between the hub and the front gate. And there was no easy way to neutralize the guards with rifles in the two towers on either side of the gate.

But one thing at a time.

They turned a corner to head toward the administrative suite of offices and nearly ran into a guard. He looked them over and started to bark at them in Turkish.

Morgan coiled and prepared to jump the guy when Conley held up a hand and said, "Let me handle this. Remember, I speak the language." He stepped forward and said something to the guard in Turkish, who turned his eyes down reflexively. Conley brought up his right fist and connected soundly to the side of the man's face.

The guard went down.

"Did you just tell him his shoelaces were untied?" Morgan asked.

Conley shrugged. "I told you it pays to learn the local language."

They raced down the hallway and turned the last corner that would take them into the administrative suites, which included the warden's office.

With luck, they would face nothing more than bureaucrats and a guy with no depth perception.

There was only fifty yards of hallway between them and the staircase that led down to the armory. But before they got two steps forward, five men stepped into the far end of the corridor, right in front of the stairs. Four of the men were guards, and big ones. Each had a night stick in his hand.

The other man Morgan recognized by his eye patch.

The warden's eye scanned them and he shouted something at them. Then his eye settled on Morgan.

"Cougar, you want to take this," Morgan said.

His partner fired off a quick reply. Morgan knew Conley's Turkish was good, nearly fluent. But he'd never pass for a native speaker.

Morgan turned to Dr. Erdem and Tunca, "Get out of here. Head to the main hallway and wait for us."

The two men started backing away, which only made the warden shout louder.

And then the warden let out something that Morgan could only describe as a scream. Morgan saw recognition in the man's remaining eye.

He was pointing at Morgan and nearly wailing.

Morgan turned to Conley and said, "What do you say, you want to take these guys?"

The partners each took a second to size up the guards. They were big and they each had their night sticks out. Plus, there was the warden. Morgan didn't love the odds.

"No," Conley said sharply.

"Me either," Morgan said, turning and racing back down the hallway. He tapped his ear comm and said, "We've got company. Do you have eyes on us?"

"Yes," Alex said. "What do you need?"

"As soon as we clear the door lock it behind us," Morgan said.

Conley was shouting instructions up ahead of them. Then Tunca and Erdem were running for the doors. They were large, steel double doors with a panel of reinforced glass on each side. They would hold against anything the warden and his buddies could throw at them, at least in the short term.

Erdem reached one of the doors first and pushed at it. It was locked.

"Shep, have you got the door?" Morgan shouted as he sprinted. If the door didn't open in a few seconds, he and Conley would slam into it.

"Working on it," Shepard said.

There was a click and then Erdem was pushing the doors open. He and Tunca stepped through just as Morgan and Conley raced out behind them.

Automatically, Morgan skidded to a stop and turned to shut the door behind him. He knew Conley was doing the same. However, before he could complete the operation, Erdem and Tunca were slamming the doors shut for them.

There was a click and a red light that told Morgan the doors were locked.

Then there was a loud thud as five men pounded on the doors at once.

They didn't budge.

Through the reinforced glass, Morgan could see that the warden was nearly bursting with rage.

"He really has to take it easy," Conley said.

"You're not kidding, stress can be a killer," Morgan said.

"You know this doesn't give us much time," Conley said.

Morgan nodded. The warden and the guards would all have cell phones. And even if there was little or no signal this far inside the hub, it was just a matter of time before word got out and the prison was locked down. And someone would reach the authorities outside, if they hadn't done so already.

"We need to get moving," Conley said.

"Sure but there's one thing I have to do first," Morgan said. He turned back to the reinforced glass and saw the warden screaming and pounding on the glass.

Morgan put his hand out, palm forward, taking care to splay out his fingers. It had been fifteen years, but Morgan was pretty sure he had executed the rude gesture correctly. The warden was shocked silent, his remaining eye going wide.

Turning, Morgan raced down the hallway, gesturing the others to follow. Behind him, he heard a new batch of pounding and screaming.

"Alex, we're heading for the garage," Morgan said.

"Even if you can get your hands on a vehicle, once the prison goes into lockdown, the guards in the tower will fire on anything leaving the hub," Alex said.

"I'm counting on it," Morgan said. "In the meantime, feel free to spread a little chaos."

* * * *

"What have you got?" Alex said to Shepard.

"I can open all of the cells—that should keep the guards busy in the cellblocks. I can also turn off the power in those areas. There will be emergency lights that operate on batteries but it will still get pretty dark in there."

"All good. If they are running around in the dark, they won't be making trouble for our team. What about water? Can you set off the sprinklers?"

Shepard thought about that for a second. "Tricky to do because they are tied to the fire alarm and we don't want fire or police here. Give me five minutes."

Alex had her own work to do. This was happening fast, and she still needed ground transport and an exfiltration scenario—not just for the team, but for herself and Shepard too.

In the original plan, there would have been time for them to change their identities and get out under different passports. Now, they couldn't leave the room while the operation was on-going. And, officially, they were the children of Dan Jackson, an American charged with terrorism who hopefully was about to become famous for escaping from prison.

"We have a problem," Shepard said.

"You mean a new one?" Alex asked.

"Yeah, someone got a message out. Local police chatter says there's something going on at Erdoğan Prison. We're keeping them pretty busy at the main Izmir Prison, but patrol cars have been dispatched."

"Can you slow them up?"

"The team at Zeta is manipulating traffic lights. We can keep them tied up in traffic and send out some fake alerts, but that will just delay arrival. Someone is going to get there sooner or later."

Work fast Dad, Alex thought.

* * * *

Once they were finished with their own equipment, Morgan and Conley helped Tunca and Erdem put on their riot gear. All four men were soon wearing black overalls, full body armor, and helmets with plastic visors that could be lowered to cover their faces.

Not only would it give them more freedom to move about the prison, but the body armor would be essential if they were going to get out of here.

When everyone was suited up, they headed out of the locker room. It wasn't much but Morgan was happy to have the weight of the night stick on his hip. He would have preferred his Walther, but the way this mission was going, he'd take what he could get.

"Let's move," Morgan said.

Conley led the team toward the front entrance as Morgan tapped his ear comm. "Who is left on the garage level?" he asked.

"Just office staff and maintenance," Shepard said through the comm.

As they reached the stairwell, water started spraying from the ceiling. "What's that?" Erdem asked.

"Just spreading a little chaos," Alex said, through the comm.

Once they were on the stairs, Morgan saw the lights go out behind them.

"Nice work, Shepard," he said, as they barreled down the stairs. "Is the warden staying put?"

"He's still there. Still pretty mad…and moist."

That made Morgan smile.

CHAPTER SIXTEEN

Rounding up the staff on the garage level was easier than Morgan had expected. The riot gear gave them authority, and Tunca's native Turkish was all they needed to convince the staff to wait out the crisis in one of the level's storage areas. Once the staff was inside, Shepard locked the door for them—giving the team the run of the entire underground parking and maintenance complex. Beside the dozens of cars owned by the staff, there were three prison buses and two ambulances.

Morgan sent Dr. Erdem and Tunca to find the keys to the official vehicles. "I don't like that look, what are you thinking?" Conley said while they were alone.

"There's no way around it, we have to drive out of here. Shepard can take care of the gate," Morgan said.

"Sure, but we have to get there. There is one military trained sharpshooter in each of those two towers out front. They will shoot at anything leaving the compound, and they won't miss."

"We're all wearing body armor and the roof of the bus will provide limited protection," Morgan said.

"You know that any high velocity round will tear right through it."

"True, but they won't be able to see us. We'll spread everyone out inside the bus and move quickly," Morgan replied.

"Of course, the driver will be the most exposed."

"Yes, but I say we give them something else to shoot at. We'll send out the ambulance first with the bus right behind."

"They'll focus on the ambulance sure, but the driver will be cut to ribbons," Conley said.

"I'll rig the ambulance to drive straight on its own, hop on the bus and off we go."

"I hate it," Conley said.

Morgan waited a few seconds.

Conley shook his head. "Obviously we don't have a choice, but just to be clear, I hate it."

"Noted," Morgan said, as Tunca and Erdem returned holding keys.

Morgan started the ambulance while Conley loaded the doctor and the journalist into the bus and got behind the wheel.

They drove up the ramp as Shepard raised the heavy steel garage door. The entrance was wide enough that the bus and the ambulance could fit side by side just inside the door.

"How are you going to make sure it drives straight? If it veers and blocks our path…" Conley said through the comm.

"I've got a plan for that," Morgan said. "Just be ready to follow my lead."

"So your plan is to drive the ambulance yourself, just to draw fire?" Conley said.

Morgan didn't respond. He put on the riot helmet, lowering the visor. The clear plastic wouldn't stop a bullet but it would protect his face from flying glass.

"Dan…" Conley started.

"You know I hate to let anyone else drive," Morgan said, flipping on the siren and the lights.

"Dan, you can't. Bag the ambulance then. We'll all take our chances in the bus."

"Not if you're driving," Morgan said. Conley's expression was somewhere between furious and horrified. "Try to keep up," Morgan added, flooring the ambulance, which lurched out of the underground parking lot and headed down the drive.

The first shot came less than two seconds after he hit the courtyard. It came from his right, through the windshield, and then slammed into the passenger seat. The next shot came from his left and he could feel it nick his helmet.

Keeping his head down, Morgan traded a little visibility for more protection from the helmet. From twenty-five feet up, it would be hard to hit his neck or face. However, it wouldn't take much luck to hit any of the joints in his upper body, where the armor was necessarily the weakest.

As soon as he had that thought, he felt a hammer slam into the right side of his chest. The ambulance lurched right and Morgan had to fight to pull it straight back to the left. He decided to pull even further in that direction. It would reduce the angle of fire from the guard tower on his left. It also put more of the ambulance between him and the guard tower on the right. The extra space would also give Conley more room to race past him and get the hell out of here.

The gate started to swing open when Morgan was less than fifty yards from it. They were almost through. He counted the reports in his head. He thought all the fire was directed at him but he wasn't sure.

Then he felt another hammer slam into him, this time into his upper left shoulder. The pain was so big and so immediate that Morgan couldn't tell if the bullet had pierced his body armor.

The blow rendered his left arm useless and almost instantly the ambulance lurched left. However, this time it hit the bottom of the guard tower before he could compensate.

The ambulance was stuck, just as the gates had fully opened.

Morgan was pleased to see the bus now had a clear run at the open gate. As long as the guards didn't get lucky, Conley and the others would all get through.

Though Morgan's left shoulder was on fire, he felt an obligation to make an effort to get out of the vehicle. If his daughter was watching, he didn't want her to see him give up.

He opened the driver's side door and slumped out. Fortunately, the guard in the left tower—which was now above him—no longer had an angle on him. Of course, the guard on the right still had a shot, which is why Morgan was trapped behind his ambulance.

He watched with satisfaction as the bus headed for the gate…

And then it stopped.

No, Morgan thought.

Conley had put his bus between Morgan and the guard tower on the right.

Sure enough, there was immediate rifle fire from that tower. Morgan wanted to move, feeling he should help.

Just then, someone grabbed him and pulled him up from his near crouch.

Morgan turned to see it was Conley, who was pulling him forward as the bus moved with them, providing limited cover. One of the prisoners must be driving, Morgan realized.

Morgan could hear gunshots hit the bus, more than one striking very close to the two agents. Human nature directed the guards to shoot for the biggest target. In moments, they would realize that they had a better shot at the two men but before that happened Morgan and Conley as well as the bus were outside the gate. It shut behind them and Morgan said a silent thanks to Shepard. The guard towers weren't open to the front, so the guards couldn't shoot down at them.

Morgan realized they were safe, at least for the moment—though the sirens in the distance told him they didn't have long.

People stopped to gawk at them. Tunca shouted at them in Turkish and they moved on.

"You okay?" Conley said, suddenly next to him, giving him a quick once-over.

Morgan was pleased to see that he was okay. His shoulder and chest throbbed but there was no blood.

"Anyone get hit?" he muttered.

"Just you," Conley said.

The others were removing their riot gear and Morgan did the same. He felt better when they were all in civilian clothes. He was in still in pain, but he was mobile and just being outside of the prison was a good feeling.

Alex's voice was suddenly in his ear, "Keep on the street you are on and walk directly away from the prison. Make your first right and you'll see your ground transport. It's a box truck; you'll know it when you see it."

Before they were half a block away, patrol cars raced past them to the prison. They made the turn and there was a brightly colored food delivery truck, painted in loud reds and oranges and emblazoned with pictures of food.

Conley laughed when he saw it. "Kurdish food."

Morgan was pleased. *Nice going, Alex.*

Conley got behind the wheel as the others filed in.

Then Alex was on the comm again. This time she sounded out of breath, as if she was on the move.

She gave them a waterfront address and said, "We'll meet you there."

By now there was a lot of police activity, with patrol cars heading in all directions. On the way, Tunca shouted something up front and pointed to CDs sitting on the console. Morgan passed them to Tunca, who shuffled them quickly and handed one back to Morgan.

As he put it in, Dr. Erdem said, "Kurdish music was banned until 1991, Perwer drives them particularly crazy."

Opening his window, Morgan turned up the sound as they drove through the streets. He couldn't tell if the truck and music were actually keeping people away from them, but the thought pleased him.

He was afraid of traffic—especially after all of the monkeying around that Shepard had done with the city's traffic lights and emergency alerts—but there weren't a lot of people on the road.

Fifteen minutes later, they were at the docks and the chaos of the prison was almost undetectable. Just the same, Morgan knew he'd feel better when they got out of the country.

Alex appeared from a black van, followed by Shepard. They were dressed in casual, dark clothes and seemed like they had had a long day. As soon as she saw him, Alex rushed up to look him over.

"Everybody okay?" she asked, focusing her attention on him.

"All present and accounted for, just a few bruises," Morgan said.

"Then let's get out of here," she said, nodding to Conley and the others. The entire group helped with the bags in the van and Alex led them to a fishing boat. One middle-aged and one young man greeted them, helping them onto the boat, which barely fit the group.

"Where we headed?" Morgan said as they got underway.

"Greece," Alex said.

Morgan took in the small fishing boat. Space aside, he doubted the boat had that kind of range. Though there were some islands a bit closer, the Greek mainland was nearly three hundred miles away.

"Don't worry, our friends are only taking us part of the way," she said, gesturing up ahead to a gleaming white ship. It was big, and when they got closer Morgan could see the Renard Tech logo on the side.

Scott Renard was the billionaire boyfriend of Zeta agent Lily Randall. More than once he'd provided Zeta with much-needed assistance.

As they got closer to the ship, which appeared to be some sort of giant corporate yacht, Morgan decided that this was the kind of assistance he could get behind.

* * * *

On the ship, Morgan learned that, aside from eight crewmembers, the Zeta team and their two rescued prisoners were the only people on board. Before the team's formal debriefing, they got a solid night's rest. Morgan was able to confirm that none of his ribs were broken under the bruises.

They'd also put on fresh clothing and enjoyed a brunch made by the ship's chef. Later, they all met up in the conference room where Shepard was preparing a teleconference with Zeta headquarters.

Morgan noted that Erdem and Tunca seemed to have become fast friends and were chatting together.

Diana Bloch's face appeared on the conference room screen and the debriefing began. After Erdem and Tunca had spoken, they were escorted out and the Zeta team made their final report.

"This mission was important and you pulled it off—despite the surprises. Thank you."

Then she frowned and Morgan knew what was coming. "However, the cost has been high. As you know, we've invested quite a bit of money and years of work into placing assets inside the Turkish prison system—which has been made much easier because of their massive construction program. Now we have probably lost access to those assets."

"Actually," Shepard said, "I think we'll be okay there."

For one of the very few times since he'd known her, Diana Bloch seemed genuinely surprised.

"We didn't have much time but O'Neal and I came up with some interesting ways to hide our operation," Shepard said. "The hacking into the prison system will now be tied to the warden's computer. We've arranged it so that even a thorough, digital forensic analysis will show that access was gained by eastern European hackers because the warden downloaded some…questionable material online."

Morgan smiled at that. "Anything extreme?" he asked.

"That depends on how you feel about tentacles," Shepard replied.

"And we were working too fast to cover all of our tracks with the city emergency and traffic systems. However, with your permission, we can tie it to the minister of energy's access codes. And just to be sure, I can arrange a transfer from an unnamed eastern European bank to his account so it will appear that he sold access and the hackers were testing the system."

That was fine with Morgan. Tunca was in prison for accurately reporting that the same minister was illegally buying oil from some of the worst terrorists on earth. Of course, he'd almost certainly done it with the approval of President Shakir.

"So our assets and access will remain in place?" Bloch said. "Good, we never know when we'll need Morgan and Conley to go back inside."

After the meeting, Alex approached Morgan alone on deck. "Daddy, I'm sorry things got so out of hand."

"Never apologize for a mission that was a complete success. And none of it was your fault. If it was anyone's, it was mine. I could have finished the job with the warden back when he was a soldier."

"I read the report. You sent him back with a warning. Who knows how much suffering that prevented."

"Maybe. And we got Dr. Erdem out. Plus, the truth will get out about Shakir's oil deals. Think of this as a lesson: no mission plan—like no battle plan—survives for long in the real world. The key is to roll with it. You and Shepard did that and we all got the job done."

Alex seemed satisfied and Morgan checked his watch. They had another six or seven hours before they reached the Greek mainland. Morgan found that he wasn't in a rush. It was a beautiful day and the chef had promised something special for dinner.

Conley took a seat on the deck chair next to him and Morgan decided to take some of his own advice. Bloch had been mostly kidding when she said they might need to send him and Conley back into the Turkish prison system. However, Morgan had been doing this for too long to rule anything out.

But right now, he was no longer on a mission. The team was safe, and he was on a ship in the Aegean with the sun shining down on them.

He decided to take the win.

Don't miss the next exciting Dan Morgan thriller

ENEMY ACTION

Coming soon from Lyrical Press, an imprint of Kensington Publishing Corp.

Keep reading to enjoy a preview excerpt . . .

Chapter 1

Twenty-Seven Years Ago

"Is it me," Peter Conley said, "or is it chilly out?"

Dan Morgan checked the thermometer built into the arm of his parka. It read: -88F. "Must be you."

"You have to factor in the wind chill," Conley said. "That makes it feel colder."

Morgan didn't think it could ever feel colder. After this mission, he resolved never to complain about Boston winters again. Of course, they could have made the trip through the station itself, but Morgan had insisted that they start spending time outside as soon as possible.

If the mission suddenly turned hot (metaphorically, if not literally) and they had to operate outside tactically, he didn't want that to be their first real experience outdoors in the cold. Plus, they could be here a week, or three months, and he figured the sooner they acclimated, the better.

The trade-off was that the time necessary to put on and then take off their parka, gloves, face mask, and goggles was much longer than the three- or four-minute walk through the hallways.

Since it challenged his sense of efficiency, Conley had complained, but not much. Besides getting used to the cold, it was good practice getting in and out of their cold-weather gear.

Entering the south doorway, Morgan and Conley were met by Walter, the young physicist who had been assigned to orient the partners to the base. Though he looked impossibly young to Morgan, at twenty-five or -six, he was a couple of years older than Morgan and Conley themselves.

But as Morgan had learned from his work with cars, it's not the years, it's the mileage. Walter had likely spent very little of his life outside of a lab. Morgan thought that was a good thing. People like himself and Peter did the high-mileage/high-wear-and-tear work so people like Walter could do the kind of research that they were doing in places like Antarctica.

"Have you talked to Dr. Russell yet?" Walter asked.

"No, but we've read up on him," Conley offered.

"So you know that his work made this research possible. In fact, he largely designed our equipment," the young man said, a clear air of respect in his voice.

"I'm looking forward to it," Morgan replied.

As they approached the open door to Russell's office, Morgan could hear movement inside. By the time they entered, Russell was at the door to meet them.

Russell was maybe sixty years old, trim, with salt-and-pepper hair and glasses. "Walter, thank you for bringing our guests," he said, holding out his hand.

Morgan shook first and said, "Dan Morgan." Conley repeated the procedure.

"Good to meet you, and I'm glad to have you here. Come in." The office was spacious and Russell led them to a small round conference table.

"Again, I'm grateful that your . . . employer sent you to us," Russell said, letting that hang in the air for a few seconds. "Even though we've been getting along fine without a pilot or a helicopter, I know we've been lucky in that we haven't had an emergency that required either."

"Then for as long as we're here, you can rest easier," Conley said.

"And though I appreciate having you both here," Russell said to Morgan, "I have to say that we really don't need an electrical systems technician."

"My attitude is that technicians are a lot like flamethrowers; better to have one and not need it than need one and not have it," Morgan said.

Russell laughed heartily.

"We hardly ever need a flamethrower down here, but we do have them, so I take your meaning; and I am truly grateful to your employer for offering your special *security* expertise," Russell said.

"The Agency is happy to help," Morgan said. That was as close as he would come to saying "the CIA," and that was fine in this company.

Russell had a relatively high security clearance, as did Walter—who had done some graduate work with lasers for a Department of Defense project.

"Why do you think the Russians have taken such an interest in you?" Conley said.

"I'm not sure. Our work in neutrino detection is pure theoretical physics. It doesn't have the sort of practical or military applications that seem to drive Russian physics research." Russell said *practical* and *military* with some distaste, but Morgan didn't begrudge the man his feelings given what he was doing out here.

It must have been unnerving to know that the Russian intelligence agencies had been watching your work for months and that the Russian military had just made the largest troop deployment in the history of Antarctica in your neighborhood.

"Do you think they might want to steal your research?" Morgan offered.

"Unlikely. We're looking into fairly esoteric and cosmic questions here. Again, I can't see them actually caring about our work."

"If they were up to something, say, a secret nuclear reactor in Antarctica, could your system detect it?" Conley asked.

Morgan could see that the man respected the question, but Russell shook his head. "There's no need. If you wanted to secretly generate massive amounts of power—presuming you had something you wanted to do with that much power—there are better ways."

"Better than a nuclear reactor?" Conley asked.

"Of course. Mt. Erebus is an active volcano and is one of hundreds under our feet. If you wanted to generate power in secret, you could build a geothermal plant that would give you as much power with less trouble and less chance of being detected."

"For now," Morgan said, "let's just assume the Russians are just being nosy, and the troop deployment is a show of force unrelated to your work. Perhaps they are thinking about renegotiating the treaty that says no single country owns this continent. There is petroleum underneath the ice here. Perhaps they have designs there and just happen to have chosen your neighborhood for their base."

Even as Morgan said it, his gut told him it wasn't true. In his experience, the Russians were strategic thinkers, and with them, unlikely events happening in proximity to one another were never a coincidence.

However, it wouldn't pay to panic the civilians. If something came up, he and Conley would have to handle it. In fact, if something *was* going to happen, Morgan would prefer that it happen sooner rather than later.

He had business of another sort with a Russian back in the States. Natasha Orlov was ready to defect, but she wouldn't do it unless he was there to see to the details personally.

She didn't trust anyone else at the Agency, and the fact was that Morgan *wanted* to be there. He also wanted to make sure she was safe, and she definitely wanted him to be there when she was debriefed.

And when all of that business was finished, they could continue the personal business they had begun at the Russian Embassy in Washington.

"As I said, I'm glad you are here, but there are only two of you. What happens if the Russian troops become aggressive? I have thirty people to worry about here," Russell said.

"I want you to leave that to the both of us. I'm a very good technician, and Mr. Conley is an excellent pilot. And there are barely two hundred of them. We'll do our job so you can concentrate on yours," Morgan said.

That seemed to satisfy Russell. It helped that the man wanted to believe him. It helped even more that Morgan meant it. Heisenberg Base was their mission now. He and Conley would do whatever it took to keep it safe.

"While you are here, I hope you will take advantage of our facilities. We do our best to make everyone comfortable. Walter can show you around," Russell said, his tone politely indicating the meeting was over.

"Actually, I wanted to get right to work and visit the Stack," Morgan said.

"You want to see the equipment?" Russell asked.

"Yes, I've seen the specs and I'm not happy with the failure rate of some of the sensors," Morgan said.

"You suspect sabotage?" Russell said.

"Not at all. I have some concerns about the power system," Morgan said.

Russell's mouth hung open, and Walter was looking at Morgan like he had just waltzed into the Vatican and challenged the pope to an arm-wrestling match.

Russell recovered quickly and said, "We have over five hundred individual sensors and less than a 2 percent failure rate. That is well within our design tolerances."

"No," Morgan corrected him. "It was less than 2 percent for the first six months. Now it's over 4 percent. It's been climbing since you added wind power to supplement your diesel generators."

"I supervised that upgrade myself. Again, we're still within tolerances. In addition, you are here for *security*," Russell said.

"True, but we like to make ourselves useful," Morgan replied. "We'll bring Walter along for the survey, and I won't make any repairs unless you approve. However, it will keep us busy and maybe we can get some more of your sensors working."

"It's not really necessary . . ." Russell began, appearing unsure for the first time since the meeting started.

Conley chimed in. "Not necessary for your current work where you are back-tracing neutrinos to their source. However, if we can get your numbers up, you can start looking at neutrino interactions. Your work identifying neutrino origins is merely confirming accepted theory. But if I read your papers correctly, you have bigger ambitions."

For a second, Morgan didn't know what Russell was going to do. Then the man did the last thing Morgan expected: he laughed.

It took Walter an uncomfortable moment to process that his boss wasn't in a rage, and the young man smiled in relief.

"If you can do that, I'll buy you both a drink," Russell said.

A few minutes later, they had loaded the equipment they needed into the helicopter that Morgan and Conley had taken from McMurdo base to Heisenberg.

Once they were inside the aircraft, Morgan noticed that Walter had put his safety belt on before Morgan was even seated.

"You know, we usually just take a Snowcat out to the detector. It's a short trip," Walter said.

"I want to get some hours on this bird," Conley said.

Morgan understood. Part of Conley's motive was similar to Morgan's own desire to get up to speed on their new environment and equipment, and part of it was the fact that Conley was excited about this particular helicopter.

Conley knew aircraft the way that Morgan knew cars. He had requested the JetRanger 206 for this mission, and the Agency had obliged. All that Morgan knew about it was that it was a Canadian civilian aircraft based on a military design.

Morgan liked that it was relatively spacious inside, with room for four plus a fair amount of cargo. He noticed that Walter did not seem impressed. In fact, he looked downright nervous.

"You okay to fly?" Morgan asked.

"I've never been in a helicopter before," Walter said.

"Just like a plane, but softer on the landing," Morgan said. "Plus, you are in good hands," he added, gesturing to Conley.

Walter watched Conley studying the controls and asked, "How long have you had your license?"

"Years, I got my pilot's license when I was in high school," Conley said as he started up the chopper.

"Helicopter license?" Walter said. Morgan was impressed. The kid was sharp and had good intuition.

"That's just a formality," Conley said, and before Walter could respond, the helicopter rose off the ground. Morgan could see that Conley had made it a soft takeoff, partly to show off and partly to avoid panicking their passenger.

Once they were in the air, Walter silently clutched the armrests of his seat and watched the horizon.

It took them less than five minutes to get to the Stack, and Conley touched down softly. He turned to give Walter a reassuring smile. "See, piece of cake."

To Walter's credit, he grinned back and seemed to relax.

Once they were on the ground outside, Walter gestured to the snow in front of them and said, "What do you think?"

Honestly, it looked like most of the flat snow plains they had seen in Antarctica. The only difference was that there was some sort of waist-high metal box every twenty yards or so.

"You don't have to say it. It doesn't look like much on the outside, but you are looking at the largest sensor system in the world. The Stack has a half-square-mile footprint and goes about a half mile down, making it effectively a twenty-eight-hundred-foot cube. Each of those boxes is the control panel for a string that holds sixty evenly spaced digital optical sensors on a half-mile-long cable, giving us over five thousand individual sensor units. And that's what allows us to see nearly invisible, charge-less, mass-less particles."

Morgan had read the briefing material and knew most of this, but he let the young scientist talk.

"Do you really think you can improve the system, Mr. Morgan?" Walter said.

"First, you can call me Dan, and second, yes I can," Morgan said, heading into the field. The control boxes were numbered and it didn't take him long to find one that was on the list of strings with bad sensors. "I'm just going to pop it open and check the capacitor," he said.

On Walter's nervous nod, Morgan opened the panel on top of the box and quickly found the capacitor. "Okay if I pull it? I brought a replacement," Morgan said.

After another even more nervous nod from Walter, Morgan pulled a new capacitor from his backpack, installed it, and turned the panel back on. There was a quick reboot procedure and then the sensor string was back on line.

Walter studied the numbers on the panel readout and then his eyes went wide. "Five of the eight inoperative sensors are back on. How . . ."

"I won't pretend to understand your equipment but you made two classic mistakes. First, you ran all of your current on a single line. That means that each sensor attaches to the current at only one point. If there's corrosion, you lose a good connection to the sensor. Easy mistake to make. It's still a problem with Chryslers."

"Chryslers?" Walter asked.

"The cars, any mechanic you ask will tell you stories about Chrysler electrical systems. Also, you have too much variation in your amperage and it degrades your capacitors. Even though the current stays within specs, you get too many ups and downs. It's like having a poor performing alternator; it wreaks havoc on electronics. And the more sophisticated the electronics, the more consistent the power needs to be. Based on what they cost, your sensors are pretty sophisticated. Upgrading your capacitors will help there. I brought enough to replace all of them. Get approval from your boss and we can knock the work out in a couple of days."

"I don't know what to say," Walter said. "Cars . . ."

"Are well-engineered combinations of mechanical, electrical, and electronic systems," Morgan said. "Come on, give us the tour."

Walter walked them through the field of control boxes to a junction box of some kind. Next to that was a four-foot satellite dish on a steel post about a dozen feet high.

"The data goes to the junction and then the dish sends it back to us at Heisenberg Base," Walter said.

Morgan could see that Conley was impressed.

"When we have some time, you'll have to explain what neutrinos tell you . . ." Conley said.

Before Conley could finish, Walter became fixated on the satellite dish. "That's odd," he said.

"What is?" Morgan replied, hearing something he didn't like in the young man's voice.

When Walter was less than six feet from the dish, he raised a gloved hand and pointed at the new addition. "That box. It wasn't there before," Walter said. "And no one could have requisitioned new equipment without me seeing it, let alone created a work order. And they definitely couldn't have installed said new equipment."

The rectangular box was green, easily standing out against the white pole and dish. It was attached to the pole just under the dish. When Morgan noticed that the box had a slight curve, alarm bells started going off in his head.

"Down!" he called out, knowing that that would be enough for Conley. Walter, on the other hand, was still apparently hypnotized by the strange device.

Morgan didn't have to take the extra seconds to read the Russian words on the back of the green box to know what it was: a MON-50 mine—a Russian knockoff of the Claymore. It was attached to a small box that Morgan assumed was an electronic trigger.

At that precise instant, Walter took another step forward, and before a plan had formed in his head, Morgan flung himself into the air, tackling the man.

The explosion followed less than a second later and Morgan felt the pressure wave pass over him as something solid hit him, hard, in the back.

As his hearing started to clear, Morgan heard Conley calling to him. "I'm okay," Morgan called back, rolling off Walter.

"What about you?" Morgan asked, getting into a kneeling position and pulling Walter up. The man was moving, shaking his head to clear it, and Morgan couldn't see any injuries.

"Can you get to your feet?" he asked, as he stood and continued to pull on Walter, who was soon standing himself.

"I'm okay," he said. "What was that?"

"A landmine," Morgan said.

"What? Why?" Walter said.

"I think it's safe to say that Heisenberg Base is now under attack," Conley said.

Morgan heard his partner sputter and say, “Dan, are you sure you are all right?”

Then Conley was pulling at Morgan’s backpack. When it was off him, Morgan saw what had caused the thump on his back. A six-inch spike of metal was sticking out of the pack.

A quick swipe of his hand over his back told Morgan that the spike hadn’t touched him. “Like I said, good capacitors . . .”

About the Author

Carolle Photography

Leo J. Maloney is the author of the acclaimed Dan Morgan thriller series, which includes *Termination Orders, Silent Assassin, Black Skies, Twelve Hours, Arch Enemy, For Duty and Honor, Rogue Commander, Dark Territory, Threat Level Alpha,* and *War of Shadows*. He was born in Massachusetts, where he spent his childhood, and graduated from Northeastern University. He spent over thirty years in black ops, accepting highly secretive missions that would put him in the most dangerous hot spots in the world. Since leaving that career, he has had the opportunity to try his hand at acting in independent films and television commercials. He has seven movies to his credit, both as an actor and behind the camera as a producer, technical advisor, and assistant director. He is also an avid collector of classic and muscle cars. He lives in Venice, Florida. Visit him at www.leojmaloney.com or on Facebook or Twitter.

Printed in the United States
by Baker & Taylor Publisher Services